To Tanvi Kant, a chuisle mo chroí.

STRIPES PUBLISHING LIMITED
An imprint of the Little Tiger Group
1 Coda Studios, 189 Munster Road,
London SW6 6AW

A paperback original
First published in Great Britain in 2021

Text and illustrations copyright
© Paul Coomey, 2021

ISBN: 978-1-78895-230-9

The right of Paul Coomey to be identified as
the author and illustrator of this work has been
asserted by him in accordance with the Copyright,
Designs and Patents Act, 1988.

Printed and bound in China.

MIX
Paper from
responsible sources
FSC® C020056

The Forest Stewardship Council® (FSC®) is a
global, not-for-profit organization dedicated to
the promotion of responsible forest management
worldwide. FSC defines standards based on agreed
principles for responsible forest stewardship that are
supported by environmental, social, and economic
stakeholders. To learn more, visit www.fsc.org

STP/1800/0304/0820

10 9 8 7 6 5 4 3 2 1

STICK BOY!

WORDS &
PICTURES
➡ PAUL
COOMEY.

LiTTLE TiGER

LONDON

This is Stick Boy, running as fast as he can.
And who is that shouting at him?

Ah, that'd be Sam.

Sam looks like a big bully. Sam IS a big bully. Sam is, in fact, the second biggest bully in the whole school.

OTHER FACTS ABOUT SAM:

SAM DISLIKES:
- Deodorant
- Cats
- Dogs
- Hats
- Skateboards
- Your shoes
- Fun

SAM LIKES:
- Shouting
- Being a school bully
- And ... er, that's about it.

So here we are in the little town of Little Town, and Sam is chasing Stick Boy.

This is not good. It's Stick's second day at a new school in a new town. This time was supposed to be different. He was supposed to leave his old problems behind (again) and start somewhere new (again). A familiar feeling grows in his belly – dark, heavy, swirling dread.

He needs a place to hide, fast.

He sprints around a corner ...

       spots a handy signpost ...

            and slips behind it.

Sam pounds past then screeches to a halt. She looks left and right, up and down, her head swivelling around like a meerkat at a disco.

Stick stands still. He holds his breath. Has he managed to escape?

Hopefully.

Wait, who's this?

Hurrah! "Stick is *saved*!" I hear you cry. An angel has arrived to rescue him!

ANGEL!

PERFECT PLAITS!

GRETCHEN

DECEPTIVE APPEARANCE

BULLY #1

"Hello, Sam," the angel says with a sneer.

Oh. This doesn't look promising.

"Er, hello, Gretchen."

"Have you forgotten our little arrangement?"

"Er, no, Gretchen."

"Err, *noo, Gretchen*," mimics Gretchen. "Well, it would appear you have. *I* am in charge of acquiring new victims and *you* handle repeat clients. Why were *you* chasing the new boy?"

"Er, I don't know, Gretchen."

"What do you mean, you don't know?" Gretchen laughs. "Did you think you'd show some initiative? Were you trying to *impress* me?"

"No, I, yes, er—"

"Zip it. We're wasting time. Now, this new boy looks a bit like a big lollipop, does he not?"

"Er, yes?"

"And what else in our vicinity, Sam, looks like a big lollipop?"

"Er … that signpost?"

"Yes, Sam, *that signpost*." Gretchen sighs.

Stick already knows the game is up. He steps out. Sam makes a lunge for him, but Gretchen stops her.

"Not so fast, Sam. I'll handle this." She steps towards Stick.

"Well, hellooo there! How do you do, dear fellow?"

This is not what Stick was expecting.

"I–I'm doing all right, thank you," he says in a quiet voice.

"Dear fellow, the correct response to the enquiry of 'How do you do?' is in fact '*How do you do?*'"

"What?" says Stick.

"Don't you mean *pardon*?" Gretchen tuts again. "I'm afraid we've got ourselves off to rather a bumpy beginning here. Allow me to introduce myself. My name is Gretchen and this is my associate, Sam. Sam and I *rule* the *school*. What, may I ask, is your name, you perfectly peculiar-looking person?"

"Stick."

"I *do* beg your pardon?"

"My name is Stick. Stick Boy."

"How perfectly preposterous. Nobody is called Stick."

"I am," says Stick.

Stick looks at the ground. He's been through this

before. His family have moved three times in as many years. You might think it's because Stick is picked on wherever he goes, but it's *actually* because Stick's mum has a super top-secret job in a super top-secret government agency. At least that's what Stick thinks. His big sister, Bella, reckons they move because the branches of Supersavers Superdiscount Superstores, where Mum works, keep closing down.

"Stick, Mick, Rick, whatever," says Gretchen. "Sam, shake him down."

Introducing: THE SAM DEVINE SHAKEDOWN!

STEP 1: GRAB!

STEP 2: SHAKE!

STEP 3: SELFIE!

Gretchen glowers. "Enough grinning! Let's see what we have here."

Everything that was in Stick's pockets now lies scattered on the ground.

Yes, pockets. Some things can't be explained easily. Stick watches, upside-down, as Gretchen pokes at:

- One black marker, fat
- One shoelace, red
- One button, blue
- Two dice, yellow with black dots
- One silver key ring, with the following attached:

  - A shiny new locker key for locker number 6161 at Little Town High School
  - A new membership card for Little Town Library
  - A Supersavers Superdiscount Superstore Kidzsaver Loyalty Card
  - A front door key to number 25 Foxhollow Drive
  - An "I Love NY" key ring from the time Grandma Boy and Grandad Boy went to New York
  - A souvenir bottle opener in the shape of a flip-flop from Lanzarote, the absolute furthest-away place that Stick has ever been, and where he wishes he was right now.

Gretchen sneers. "Ugh. Sam, dispose of these *trinkets*."

Sam drops Stick into a puddle and scoops up his belongings. She spots a very high wall topped with some particularly nasty-looking spikes. She's about to throw everything over the wall when—

"*STOP!*" shrieks Gretchen. "Hand me those dice. I do believe I may find a use for them."

Then, like a champion bowler, Sam runs, grunts, swings her arm over her head and chucks Stick's keys and cards and everything else high into the air and over the wall.

"That's going to look *ace* on Vidwire," Sam says.

Gretchen smirks. "If, of course, it had been recorded."

"You didn't—?"

"Well, you didn't *ask* anyone to record it, did you? Silly old Sam."

Sam looks hurt but Stick doesn't see. He's sitting on his bum in the puddle, staring down at his reflection in the grimy water.

"Ta-ta then, Stick Boy!" And with that, Gretchen scoots off down the hill towards school, Sam thumping along behind.

Stick Boy sits.

And sits.

His throat feels tight. His eyes feel hot and prickly.

His tears plop into the puddle and swirl like ink in the grey water.

He had hoped it would be different this time. A school without the old problems. A new start.

In the surface of the puddle, Stick sees the reflection of a boy.

No, not *himself*. Another boy.

"Hello," says the boy.

"Hello," says Stick.

The boy looks about his age, with messy brown hair, brown eyes and a big smile. He has a football under his arm. He's holding out a hand to Stick.

In it are:

- One shoelace, red
- One button, blue

"Are these yours?" he asks.

"Yes," says Stick.

"I'll help you up," says the boy, putting down the football and pulling Stick to his feet. "You're heavier than you look. I'm Ekam."

"I'm Stick."

"Cool name."

"Thanks. I didn't pick it, my mum and dad did. Aren't you in our school?"

"Yeah, it's my second day," Stick says.

"Sorry about your keys and stuff. Sam's got a pretty good throw."

"Did you see where she threw them?"

Ekam nods towards the high wall. He hands Stick the button and the shoelace. "These fell before they reached the wall. I think the wind caught them."

"Thanks."

"Are you not worried about your stuff?"

"Not really." Stick looks up at the spikes on top of the wall. "This isn't the first time."

It's not even the second time. Or the third.

"Do you still have your locker key?"

"No, but I have a little trick for that." Stick smiles.

"Whoa! *How did you—*" Ekam is the first to speak, but Nic interrupts him.

"That was UNBELIEVABLE! What the...? Do mine!"

"Easy, Nic. Give the kid a minute," says Ekam. "How ... how is that even possible?"

Stick wipes his forehead and looks at the open locker. He grins. "I don't really know. It's like, if I concentrate really hard, I can change myself. Just a bit. Like the ends of my arms. Or my feet."

"What about ... your head?" Ekam asks.

Stick hesitates. He's not used to this kind of attention. "Er, yeah. My head too. Sometimes I can—"

The bell rings for assembly. The boys pick up their things and file into the school hall, and Stick relaxes a little. He feels safer in a crowd. If he ducks a bit, he doesn't stick out.

Stick out.

Staring doesn't bother Stick. He's used to it. Being pushed around does though. He thinks about the encounter with Sam and Gretchen and feels the heavy swirls in his belly again.

"Um, are you OK?" Nic says. "You look ... um ... smaller?"

"Yeah, I'm OK," Stick replies. Before he has to explain himself, the head teacher bounds on to the stage.

LOVES BEING ON STAGE

FIRM BUT FAIR

MISS O'LEARY (THE HEAD)

WELCOME, WELCOME, WELCOME, EVERYBODY! WELCOME, WELCOME, WELCOME TO DAY TWO OF TERM!

"As you know, next Saturday is a *very* special day – the Grand Official Opening Ceremony Concert at Baron Ben's Bargain Binz Magnificent Mega Mall!"

Stick can feel the excitement of the students grow. He whispers to Ekam. "What's—"

"STUDENTS!" cries the head. "A talented group of singers from our *wonderful* school will represent the young people of Little Town at the Grand Official Opening Ceremony Concert. But who will it be? This Friday, the talented winner will be chosen by …
JONNY VIDWIRE HIMSELF!"

"I'm guessing … neither of you are finalists in the competition?" says Stick.

They laugh in unison.

"The Friday Factor? No way," says Nic. "Ekam's *girlfriend* is though."

"She's not my girlfriend," says Ekam, rolling his eyes.

"Who are you talking about?" Stick asks.

"Her," says Nic, nodding to a girl on the other side of the hall. "Alannah."

"Ekam has had a crush on her since about 1997," Nic adds.

Ekam glowers. "Shut up, Nic. Seriously."

"What*ever*," says Nic. "See you losers at lunch."

"Have you really had a crush on her since before you were born?" Stick asks.

Ekam smiles. "Maybe not *that* long. She is cool though." He looks at his timetable. "Ugh, science with Birdy. What do you have first?"

"Science with Mr Jansari. Do you know where room 420 is?"

"Yep, and it's miles away – it's in the big ugly building by the sports field. Run, unless you want to be late. Although Jansari's all right, I have him for ICT. See you at lunchtime?"

Stick smiles. "Um, yeah! And … thanks again for this morning."

"That's OK, buddy, I know how it goes."

Buddy? Stick smiles again.

Stick is lost. He found the big ugly building easily enough, but it's a total maze inside.

He pulls his journal from his bag and unfolds the map.

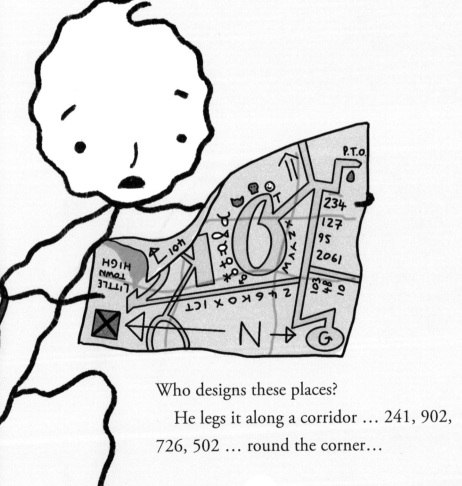

Who designs these places?

He legs it along a corridor ... 241, 902, 726, 502 ... round the corner...

"Whooooa! Hold up," says the man he's crashed into, catching Stick's head in mid-air. "What's the rush?"

"Sorry, sorry, sorry, sorry, I'm late for science and—"

"Easy, easy – I'm Mr Jansari, the science teacher, and I'm late too." He smiles. "Right. Now. First, breathe." He looks down at the bundle of sticks on the floor. "Then tell me – how does this work?"

Stick lets out a small sigh of relief. "I can do it." He sniffs. "Just put my head there, next to that long bit."

"OK," says Mr Jansari, gently placing Stick's head on the floor. "Now what?"

"Now I do this," says Stick.

Stick sticks himself back together:

1: Attach arm 2: Attach body 3: Attach arm 4: Attach legs

He stands up and picks up his bag.

"Interesting," says Mr Jansari, looking impressed. "Are we ready?"

"Yes," says Stick.

Science is Stick's absolute favourite subject. He takes a
seat at an empty desk near the back of the class and looks
around. Neither Gretchen nor Sam are here.

Suddenly the door bursts open and a very flustered
boy runs in.

"Sorry, sir! Hi, sir!"

Mr Jansari nods. "Good of you
to join us, Milo. Please take a seat."

Milo plonks himself next to
Stick and whispers, "All right?
You're the new kid, aren't you?
I'm Milo." He sticks out
a sweaty hand and Stick
shakes it.

"OK, future scientists, settle
down," says Mr Jansari. "I know you're all excited
about the Friday Factor..." The class whoops and cheers.
"Yes, very exciting, of course. The winner will sing in
the Baron's big new shop, and everybody can go there
and buy something they don't need. Won't that be fun?"
He looks around the room. "Right. Now. Enough about

DUDE

**LOVES A
GOOD WORD**

MILO

megalomaniac barons. Let's talk about racing cars, electrons, slingshots and satellites – what do all these things have in common?"

Stick has no idea. Neither does anyone else in the classroom.

As Mr Jansari explains the principles of circular motion, Stick settles in. He enjoys the satisfaction of working out equations, and he loves that the same equations can apply to things as small as atoms and as big as spaceships. He stops thinking about the bullies, and by the time the bell rings, he feels better.

Six-and-a-half minutes later...

The better feeling doesn't last. Third period is double ICT and the computer lab is all the way across the school. Stick arrives late, again, and Miss Bird is less than impressed when he knocks on the door.

"Good of you to join us. You must be Stick."

"Yes, Miss Birdy, er – Bird."

Miss Bird arches an utterly unimpressed eyebrow over her glasses. "You're late. Get *stuck*, did you?"

"It's my second day, miss, and I—"

"I don't care. Sit. And do *not* make a habit of arriving late to my classroom. You are *not* special."

That dark, swirling feeling comes creeping again. Stick tries to ignore it and walks to the back of the class, head down.

He sits at an empty desk, takes out his books and stares out of the window. The glass is frosted but he follows the blurred shapes of a pair of crows as they wheel and flap in the grey sky. He imagines being able to fly too, to lift his feet from the floor of the classroom and kick his legs and soar out of the window, slowly rising until he's high enough to see over the tops of the bare branches of the trees by the park... The sound of laughing, and of Miss Bird rapping her knuckles hard on her desk, brings his attention back to the classroom.

"Stick! Yoo-hoo!" calls Miss Bird. "Can you answer my question?"

"I don't know, miss."

"You. Don't. Know. Because you weren't listening. Alannah?"

"Yes, miss. URL stands for Universal Resource Locator."

As Miss Bird turns to the whiteboard, Alannah catches Stick's eye and gives him a sympathetic smile. He nods in return but the dark, swirling feeling stays.

Forty-eight. Minutes. Later.

By the time the bell rings for lunch, Stick is exhausted from the effort of paying attention to VPNs and SQLs. It's not like science, where he can see in his head how things fit together. The codes and scripts in ICT all look the same to him – random letters and numbers, and odd bits of punctuation. It didn't help that Miss Bird seemed to enjoy picking on him.

He keeps his head down all the way to the canteen, where he picks up a tray and shuffles along in the queue. The chef recognizes him from the day before and smiles.

"You all right, luvvie? You hungry?"

Stick nods enthusiastically. She piles his plate high with mashed potato, and smothers the pile with a rich, creamy spinach and mushroom sauce. "There you go, eat up."

Stick smiles. Then he hears his name being shouted across the canteen.

"OI! STICK!"

Oh no.

He tenses, expecting the worst, but it's Nic standing on a chair, grinning and waving.

"STIII-IICK! YOO-HOO!"

Stick breathes out. OK. This is good.

At the table, Nic is telling Milo about Stick's locker-opening trick, and Milo is listening with his mouth open. Stick says hello and starts to wolf down his food. Then Ekam arrives and plonks himself next to Stick.

"All right, bozos? All right, Stick, I see you've lost your appetite."

Stick grins and nods, his cheeks full of mashed potato.

Milo looks at Stick. "So ... what else can you do?"

"Yeah," says Ekam, "What were you saying about your head earlier?"

Sticks laughs as he finishes his potato. "Ha ha, yeah, one sec."

"That's so cool!" says Nic.

"How long does it stay like that?"

Stick is used to being the centre of attention, but he's not used to enjoying it. He smiles. "A few minutes usually. I—"

"Oh, *hello* there."

Well, look who's here. It's Gretchen, sneering like a constipated pony, and Sam lurking behind her.

"Oh, hellooooo, Gretchen," says Nic. "Come to tell us all about your dad's new shop again?"

"I beg your pardon? No, I— Actually, Knickerless, it is not a *shop*, it is a *mall*. A Magnificent *Mega* Mall.

And no. Just offering a friendly little greeting to our new schoolmate here." She gives Stick a fake smile. "Everything tickety-boo, *friend*?"

Stick squirms.

"Managing not to *stick out* too much?"

"Yes," says Stick in a small voice.

Nic leans in. He whispers to Stick, "You OK, mate? Only you've gone a bit, er … wobbly?"

Stick feels the prickling in his eyes *again*. He squeezes them shut, as tight as he can. He doesn't want to cry for a third time today.

Gretchen leans in, so close that he can smell her cheesy breath. "Well? Anything else to say for yourself? Perhaps you'd like to tell us all why you're starting school here in the middle of the year?"

That is not a question that Stick wants to answer.

Why is she picking on him? He feels something hot in his chest. It's his anger, small and burning and fierce. He's angry about letting himself be picked on. He's angry at mean Miss Bird and angry at Sam and angry at Gretchen and all her stupid questions. It's all too much. He can't—

He can't—

He snaps.

The boys are on their feet in a flash.

"Leave it, mate, she's not worth it," says Milo.

"And I'm NOT YOUR FRIEND!" shouts Stick.

"Easy, it's OK," says Nic.

Gretchen steps back, shrieking, "SAM!"

Sam grins at the boys. "Who wants to go first?"

"Go first at *what*, Sam?" asks Mr Jansari.

Where did he come from?

"Er…" splutters Sam.

"Yes?"

"Errr…"

Chop chop, Sam. Think fast.

Sam thinks. She frowns. The frowning helps with the thinking. Don't believe it? Try it yourself. Sam frowns harder:

"Vox pop, sir!"

Mr Jansari asks, "Vox pop?"

"Yes, sir, vox populi – gathering public opinion as informal comments."

Mr Jansari crosses his arms. "I know what a vox pop is, Sam, thank you. Right." He sighs and raises an eyebrow. "What about?"

"About the Friday Factor, sir!"

"I think you should begin at that table." He points across the canteen to where Alannah is sitting.

"Yes, sir."

As he leaves, Milo nods to Sam. "Nice save."

Sam smiles. "Thanks."

Gretchen shrieks. "ZIP IT, LOVEBIRDS! *Nice save.* Ugh. Revolting!"

"Everything OK, Gretchen?" calls Mr Jansari. "Why don't you run and help Sam?"

Jolly Olde English

Last period is English. Stick's late again, of course.

"Welcome!" says Mr Bell. "Stick – isn't it? I mean to say, you must be Stick. A fitting name. Class?"

They reply in unison. "Hi, Stick!" Stick shrinks a bit. "Take a seat, dear boy. There, next to Alannah."

MR BELL

LOVES TO TEACH

REGULAR CHUCKLER

Flute Snout
Snug Quince
Puck

Stick looks at the empty seat in the front row.

Gulp. He heads for his seat and opens his book, *A Midsummer Night's Dream*. He makes a face when he sees the text.

Mr Bell chuckles. "The language may seem confusing at first, but just let the words wash over you –" he makes a gesture with his hands, like the conductor of an orchestra – "and their meaning will become clear. Six volunteers, please, to read the lines!"

Loads of hands go up, but Stick's stays down.

Alannah whispers to him, "Don't you want to have a go?"

Stick shakes his head quickly and sits lower in his seat.

The scene begins, and as his classmates wrangle with the lines in old-fashioned English he tries to picture the scene in Athens. It's about some ancient men and women pleading with some old duke about who should marry who. By the time the class ends, his head is a tangle of names and arguments.

"Thank you, my fine actors!" calls Mr Bell. "See you all tomorrow for scene two!"

"That was fun!" says Alannah.

"I'm a bit confused," says Stick.

"I don't understand a lot of it either," Alannah says, "but I like the characters. See you tomorrow?"

"Yeah," says Stick. "See you tomorrow." He shuffles out with the rest of the class and spots Ekam loitering in the corridor.

"Hey, Ekam."

"Hello, Stick! How was Belly?"

Stick looks at Ekam as Alannah passes by. "A bit confusing. You weren't waiting for me, were you?" he says. They amble towards the exit with the crowd of students.

"Er, no. Sort of," says Ekam. He watches Alannah as she goes. "Listen, me and the others are going into town on Thursday after school to check out Gretchen's dad's new mall. Do you want to come?"

"Really?"

"It's not finished yet but some of the shops are open. It's got a massive satellite dish on the roof. Milo said you're a bit of a space nerd, so we thought you might like to check it out."

"OK. Let me ask my mum."

"Awesome. What are you doing now?" asks Ekam as they reach the school gates. "We're going to the park for a kickabout if you want to join in?"

"Er…" Stick hesitates. He's spotted Gretchen and

Sam lurking at the end of the road.

Ekam notices. "Ah, those two. You can handle them!"

Stick looks deflated. "I-I'm not sure I can. Today was … a lot. I think I'll head home. See you tomorrow, Ekam."

Ekam nods. "We play here every Saturday anyway. See you tomorrow, buddy."

"All right, sis?"

Bella looks up and grins. "Hey, doofus." She pulls off her headphones and Stick hears some faint guitar music. "How was day two?"

"Fine," Stick lies. "What are you doing out here? It's freezing!"

Bella points a finger in the air and leans her head to one side. "Listen," she says.

Stick listens. He hears a door slam inside the house. Then voices. It's Mum and Dad. They're shouting at each other. Again.

"Oh no," says Stick. "What are they—"

"Shh!" says Bella. "Listen."

He hears Mum's voice. "I CAN'T BELIEVE YOU'VE DONE THIS AGAIN, SIMON! DON'T YOU GET IT?"

Dad says something in reply, but it's too quiet for Bella and Stick to hear. Bella pats the wall and Stick hops up beside her. She puts an arm round him, and he leans his head on her shoulder.

"What's it about this time?" he asks.

Before she can answer, the front door opens and Dad emerges, carrying a massive cardboard box with a Baron Ben's Bargain Binz logo on it.

"Hello, bambinos," he says. "Want to see our new TV?"

Stick and Bella look at him and hesitate.

"Don't you *dare* try to get them on your side, Simon Boy," Mum says. "Hi, kiddos, how was school?"

"Fine," shrugs Bella.

"Fine," mumbles Stick.

"I'm glad you had a good day!" says Mum. "Because while you two were at school, your dad was at Baron Ben's Bargain Binz spending money we don't have on a TV we don't need!" She looks at Stick's dad. "That stupid Mega Mall is going to put me out of a job, Simon!"

"But it was a proper good deal, Anna!" says Dad. "And it came with a free HomeBot!"

"Stop going on about the HomeBot. It's just another stupid gadget for you to get bored of!" shouts Mum. Then she stops. She looks at Bella and Stick. "Sorry, chickens. Come inside, it's too chilly for you to be out here."

Let's eat!

Dinner is one of Stick's favourites but he's not enjoying it. He's trying to avoid talking about his day by not saying anything at all.

"All right, Stick?" asks Mum.

"Yes, Mum," says Stick.

"Was everything OK at school?"

Stick nods. "I ate too much at lunch." A small lie. "The dinner lady gave me extra."

"Result," says Dad.

"Aw, that was nice of her," says Mum enthusiastically. "Who did you sit with in the canteen?"

Stick sits a bit straighter and looks up from his plate. "Nic, whose locker is next to mine, Milo, who's in science with me, and another boy called Ekam."

Mum and Dad both look at Stick, mouths open.

Bella looks up from her phone. "Stop staring at him, you two. How did you meet Ekam then?"

"Just … on the way to school," Stick says.

Mum jumps up from her chair, leans over and plants a big sloppy kiss on Stick's head. "I am SO proud of you!" she squeals.

Then Dad leans over and ruffles his hair. "Good lad," he says. "Three new pals already, and only on your second day, eh?"

Stick twirls his spaghetti around and forks some into his mouth.

"All right, family?" says Dad. "Ready for an incredible, sensational, wonderful new television-viewing experience?"

Mum rolls her eyes. "Just turn the thing on, Simon."

"OK," says Dad. "Watch this."

Dad smiles. "Isn't he cute? Hey, Homie, turn on TV!"

"OK, DAD!" says the HomeBot, **"Turning on BBBBTV!"**

The TV comes on waaaaaay too loud, blaring out an ad for the new Mega Mall.

"SIMON!" shouts Mum, covering her ears. "TURN IT DOWN!"

"HEY, HOMIE!" shouts Dad. "TURN DOWN TV!"

"OK, DAD!" says the HomeBot. **"Turning on BBBBTV!"**

"FORGET SUPERSAVERS SUPERDISCOUNT SUPERSTORE! BARON BEN'S BARGAIN BINZ MAGNIFICENT MEGA MALL IS THE ONLY PLACE TO BE ON SATURDAY NIGHT! ON ANY NIGHT! BARGAINS GALORE IN STORE! MEET ME IN PERSON!" shouts Jonny Vidwire from the TV.

"HEY, HOMIE!" shouts Dad, "TURN OFF TV!"

"OK, DAD!" says the HomeBot. **"Turning up BBBBTV!"**

"THAT'S RIGHT, FOLKS!" says Jonny, grinning at the camera. "ME, JONNY-ONNY-ONNY, THE ONE AND ONLY, THE LEGEND, THE PERSON, IN PERSON, HERE IN LITTLE TOWN TO MEET MY ADORING FA—"

Mum gets up and rips the plug from the wall. She glares at Dad. "Great. Incredible. Sensational." She sighs. "I'm going to go on the laptop in the kitchen and I do *not* want to hear the TV again, so either figure out how to turn it down or don't turn it on at all!" She closes the door behind her.

"What did you think, kids?" whispers Dad.

"I think you'd better not talk to Mum until she calms down," says Bella, without looking up from her phone.

Stick sits quietly on the couch between his sister and his dad. He thinks about everything that happened during the day. The HomeBot is on the floor by his feet, its little blue lights glowing. The dark, heavy, swirling feeling inside Stick wants his attention. He gets up from the couch. The lights on the HomeBot blink when Stick moves.

"Does anyone want tea?" he asks.

Bella doesn't reply.

"Good lad, I'll have a cup," says Dad, without looking up from the instruction manual for the TV. "See if there's any bickies, eh?"

The HomeBot follows Stick. "Um, is it meant to do that?" says Stick.

"Eh?" says Dad. "Yeah, I think that's a function, let me check…"

Mum looks up and smiles when she sees Stick. "All right, twiglet? Close the door, will you, please? I don't want to hear that racket again."

Stick stands by Mum while he waits for the kettle.

He looks at the small screen of their ancient laptop. "What are you doing?"

"Oh, just some job applications."

"Are things quiet in the world of super secret agents? Hey, are you thinking of becoming a *double* agent?"

"Ha ha, very good!" says Mum. "How about a *double* double agent, so that I can still be one of the good guys?"

The kettle clicks off and Stick gets the mugs from the cupboard. The HomeBot follows him, scuttling across the lino and bumping over the cracked bit in the middle.

"I'm really proud of you, you know?" says Mum. "You'll tell me, won't you, if anyone bothers you?"

Stick pours the water into the mugs. "Yes, Mum," he says, without turning around. Another little lie.

"Thank you, poppet," says Mum. "Oh, blast it!"

"What's up?" says Stick.

"The laptop crashed again. Argh, it's that stupid robot – it pulled out the power cable! **SIMON!**"

Dad comes in. "What's up, love?"

"Can you please take that thing away before I recycle it?"

"OK, love, sorry! Thanks for the tea," he says, picking up the HomeBot with one hand and taking his mug from

Stick with the other. "Do you want to come and help me figure out this TV?"

"No thanks, Dad, I'm tired. I think I'll take my tea upstairs and read. Night, Dad. Night, Mum."

"Right you are, lad. Night night then."

"Goodnight, twiglet."

OI! STICK BOY!

STIIIIICK BOY!
STICKEDDY-STICKEDDY-
STICKEDDY-STICK
BOOOOOOY!

Oh no! It's Sam, galloping towards Stick and grinning like a barracuda. And here's Gretchen, scooting along beside her. Run, Stick!

But Stick doesn't run. This time, he's ready to face the bullies.

He looks at Gretchen. He looks at Sam. He takes a huge, deep breath then holds his nose.

In a second, he's taller than Sam.

She looks up at him in alarm.

In another second, he's as tall as a truck.

Gretchen takes a step back.

In three seconds, he's as tall as a house.

"Stick!"

Who's that?

"Sti-iick!"

He looks around for the owner of the voice. He leans down towards the town square. Who is it? Is that … Mum?

"Stick! Come on, time to go."

She reaches out and taps him on the nose. "Come on, twiglet, time to get up."

"Bye, doofus!" calls Bella through a mouth full of pancakes as she grabs her bag and rushes out of the door. "Bye, Mum, bye, Dad!"

"Bye, love!" calls Mum. "Stick, hurry up or you're going to be late, petal."

"Yes, Mum," yawns Stick as he plods downstairs.

"Here, take one with you." She hands him a pancake with chocolate spread folded into a little triangular parcel, kisses him on the cheek and pushes him out of the door. "Go, go, go!"

Dad is in the driveway, fiddling with something under the bonnet of the van. "Bye, Dad!"

"Bye, lad, have a good 'un!"

Stick walks out of the estate and round the corner. He looks out over the town. Day three. It's sunny, but cold enough to see your breath.

He takes a bite of his pancake and heads down the hill. Past the boarded-up butcher's and the closed-down bakery, over the canal bridge and then across the road that turns right and goes to Mum's work. He walks along the line of trees that look like witches.

He imagines the trees pulling up their roots and stomping through the town square, crushing cars and cackling in their witchy way.

He remembers his dream. He remembers how *angry* he felt. He remembers how Gretchen and Sam screamed. Gretchen and Sam. He hasn't seen them yet, but he's not taking any chances. He sees the park ahead of him and decides to take the long way round, just in case.

He can just about see the school in the distance, and hear the shouts of the arriving students. He wanders on slowly, thinking more about the day before. The noise grows quieter as he walks. And then he hears something else. A faint ringing. He pokes at his ear. What *is* that? A bell? The assembly bell! Oh no!

Stick tosses his bag over the park fence, then slips between the bars and legs it, through some bushes and up a little hill.

Stick runs as fast as he's ever run before, bounding over dog poo, old newspapers and takeaway cartons. He scatters a flock of pigeons and splashes through the boating pond (no shoes to get wet!), through the playground, past the café and the rose garden and now he's almost at the school and … the gates are shut.

He throws his bag over the gates, turns sideways, ducks a little and slips between them. Through the tall windows of the assembly hall he can see Miss O'Leary on stage.

Crouching as low as he can, he scurries to the entrance. The doors are still open. No teachers in sight. Suddenly he hears footsteps, and a voice he recognizes. It's Miss Bird!

He stashes his bag by a bin and steps into the dusty space behind a row of lockers, putting his foot in half an ancient cheese sandwich. Grim. He fights the urge to sneeze.

Miss Bird is getting closer. Who is she talking to? Is she on the phone?

"Yes, sir. Sorry, sir. I know I can find a solution." This does not sound like the Miss Bird from yesterday. There's a wobble in her voice. She sounds … *frightened*?

"I know we have a deadline… Yes, sorry, *I* have a deadline. Yes, I know what's at stake. Yes, on Saturday. I'll be ready. I—" She stops talking abruptly, like the person on the other end has hung up.

The dust behind the lockers is really tickling Stick's nose now, and if he doesn't sneeze soon his head is going to explode. Stick squeezes his face to try to stop the sneeze.

Suddenly the bell rings and the hallway is filled with children tumbling out of assembly and making their way to first period. In the noise and commotion, Stick sneezes without being heard. The relief! The snots! Ugh. He quietly slips out and joins the crowd.

Stick finds his way to maths without bumping into Gretchen and Sam, but he doesn't see any of his new friends either. He goes to the school secretary after second period to get a new key for his locker, but by the time he's done pretending he doesn't know how he lost the key and filled in all the forms the bell is ringing for English and he has to leg it, again.

Mr Bell is already scribbling on the board when Stick arrives, and he tries to slip into his seat unnoticed.

"Stick!" Mr Bell says. "How good of you to join us! I mean to say, do try not to make a habit of being late, dear boy."

Stick hears chuckles behind him and sinks lower in his seat.

"Don't worry about it," whispers Alannah. "He's said the same thing to most of us. Big fan of punctuality."

Stick gives a small nod. He squints to read Mr Bell's terrible handwriting:

Act 1 Scene 2

Mr Bell turns and claps his hands together happily. 'So! Today we find ourselves in the house of Peter Quince, where Quince is choosing the actors for his play-within-a-play, *The Most Lamentable Comedy and Most Cruel Death of Pyramus and Thisbe.*"

Stick opens his book to see that none of the characters from the first scene take part in the second one. He sighs.

"Yes, Stick? Are you volunteering to read a part?"

"Er, no, I—"

"Splendid! Let's see – how about you read the part of Bottom?"

"Bottom, sir?" says Stick.

"Yes, Stick. Nick Bottom."

As Mr Bell chooses volunteers to read the other parts, Stick reads some of Bottom's lines to himself. He recognizes some of the words and tries not to be nervous. He can do this.

"Alannah, you will read the part of Flute and I will read the part of Quince," says Mr Bell, with a clap. He looks at the class over his glasses. "Let us begin! Ahem… Is all our company here?"

Silence. Alannah nudges Stick. Gulp.

"Ah, sorry, sir," Stick coughs. He reads the line. "You were best to call them generally, man by man, according to the … scrip."

There's muttering in the back of the room, and a voice says, "Can't hear, sir!"

"Yes, quite," says Mr Bell. "Stick, dear boy, I must ask you to project!"

"Project, sir?" says Stick.

"Yes, yes, project," booms Mr Bell. "I mean to say, make your voice heard. Imagine yourself on the stage of Shakespeare's Globe Theatre, in front of three thousand noisy revellers. The ones at the back of the audience won't hear you, and soon they'll be flinging lumps of bread and bits of mouldy old fruit at you. Try the line again, and this time give it some oomph!"

Stick nods. He takes a deep breath.

"YOU WERE BEST TO CALL THEM GENERALLY MAN BY MAN ACCORDING TO THE SCRIP."

"Bravo!" says Mr Bell as the class laughs. "Much better. Perhaps slightly *less* oomph? Somewhere in between?"

Stick nods. It felt good to raise his voice. Being loud made him feel … bigger?

Mr Bell interrupts his thoughts. "Let us continue. Here is the scroll of every man's name…"

Stick doesn't fully understand what he's saying, but Mr Bell interrupts to explain the lines as they go. In the scene they're reading, Bottom seems to want to play every part, and comes up with more and more ridiculous reasons why he'd be the best actor for each role. Bottom loves being the centre of attention. The scene is funny and as it goes on Stick finds that he's actually looking forward to reading his next lines and hearing the laughter that follows. When the bell rings Mr Bell shouts over the noise of hungry children rushing to pack up and get to the canteen. "Class! Before you go, a round of applause for our players today, please! Players, take a bow!"

Stick turns round and bows with Alannah and Mr Bell.
He grins at the sound of clapping and cheering. This is
different. This is good.

6 ONE LITTLE THING

The good feeling doesn't last. Five minutes later Stick is stuck with Sam in the canteen. Her plate is already clean, and she's spooning the last of her apple crumble and custard into her gob.

Stick pushes his plate across the table to Sam. At least the hunger growling in his belly muffles the dark, heavy feeling a bit. He stands up.

"Sit," growls Sam.

Stick sits.

He looks down at the table. He hears a screechy whine and the quick crack of hard shoes against the floor as Gretchen marches towards their table.

"SAM! What is the meaning of this? You were scheduled to meet me—"

She stops. She's spotted Stick.

"Well! Helloooo there, my sticky friend!" She grins. "Just the fellow I wanted to see! I have a very special job for you, my new chum!"

Stick tries to reply. His words come out quietly. "I'm not your fr—"

Gretchen leans in. "I beg your pardon?" Her voice is soft and threatening. "Listen to me, Boy. Do a little something for me and then we'll leave you alone. One little thing. Of course, if you choose not to then we will make your days very, very difficult indeed."

Stick glances up at Sam, who cracks
her knuckles and glares at him.

Stick nods.

Gretchen claps. "Excellent.
That's all settled then. Meet us
outside the science lab after fifth
period." The bell rings. "Oh my,
is it that time already? Places to go, pupils
to persecute. Until this afternoon then, old chap," chirps
Gretchen. Sam grunts.

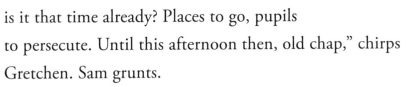

Stick sits while the canteen empties. When he's the
only one left, he picks up his bag and walks slowly to
class.

Later...

Last period of the day is science. Stick manages to find his
way there without getting lost, and when he gets to the
lab, Mr Jansari is writing something on the board and the
rest of the students are on their feet, so he gets to his seat
unnoticed.

"Dude!" says Milo, high-fiving Stick. "What's up? We
missed you at lunchtime."

"Hey," says Stick. "I was in the canteen. Where were you guys?"

"Having a kickabout outside. Here." He hands Stick some string and a ping-pong ball.

"Thanks," says Stick. He holds up the ball and the string. "Mini me?"

Milo chuckles.

"Right, now," calls Mr Jansari. "You should all have a ball and some string. Yesterday we talked about the theory of circular motion and today we're going to demonstrate the principles. Safety goggles on."

Stick gets lost in a world of centripetal force and tangential velocity and slowly forgets about what happened in the canteen. By the time the bell rings, the class are whirling the ping-pong balls above their heads. Milo has utterly mastered the concept of tangential velocity and is using his newfound skill to land his ping-pong ball in the left eye socket of the lab skeleton.

"Thank you, class," calls Mr Jansari above the ruckus. "Thank you." The class quietens down. "Bring your equipment to the front as you leave, please. See you all on Friday."

"What are you doing now?" asks Milo as they walk towards their lockers.

"Heading home," says Stick.

Has he forgotten something?

"Cool," says Milo. "I'm gonna run, I have football practice."

"See ya," says Stick.

Stick feels pretty happy as he heads towards the school doors. He likes the feeling of looking forward to seeing his friends the next day.

Guess who's about to show up and ruin things?

"Can you put me down?" asks Stick.

"Better if I don't," mutters Sam. "For both of us."

"What do you mean?" asks Stick.

"Nothing. Shut it," barks Sam.

"Quiet, you two," hisses Gretchen. She looks around. "Put him down, Sam."

Sam does as she's told. They're outside the science lab. It's empty and the lights are off inside.

"Here we are," says Gretchen. "I was most impressed by

your little trick with the lockers yesterday. Such a useful talent. So here's what's going to happen: you are going to do whatever-that-weirdo-thing-it-is you do with the end of your arm and unlock this door. Now."

Stick steps towards the door and then hesitates. He knows this is wrong. Very wrong.

"Am I sensing some uncertainty?" asks Gretchen. "Do allow me to be of assistance. Here are your options:

"Option one: You unlock the door and we won't pick on you any more – we call it quits and everyone is home in time for tea.

1

"Option two: My associate here detaches your arm at the shoulder and we attempt to use it to pick the lock ourselves. Since she has little experience in this area, I daresay the results may be … *messy.*

2

"Option three…" She moves closer to Stick, whispering now. "You run along home. And then this evening Mummy Stick will open her dreadful old laptop to read an anonymous message. Didn't have a very good time at your last school, did you?"

3

Stick gulps. The dark, heavy swirls grow.

"Didn't think so. I'll bet you've gone home and told Mummy and Daddy all about your lovely new friends.

They must be thrilled! But I'll bet you haven't told Mummy and Daddy about your little run-in with us, have you? They would be ever so disappointed to hear that their little twiglet has let himself be pushed around. All. Over. Again.

"Instead you've lied to them and told them that everything is tickety-boo. Isn't that right? So today, Sticky Boy, if you don't do as Gretchen says, Mummy Stick will find out the truth about your new start and she'll know you lied to her." Gretchen makes a sad face. "And Mummy doesn't like it when her little one lies to her, does she? It makes her so *sad*. So *disappointed*."

Stick doesn't reply. How has Gretchen guessed all of this? And how the flip does she know how old their laptop is? She's right though. Stick's mum does not like lying. How many little lies has he told her already?

He steps towards the door and lifts up his arm.

"After this we're quits, right?" says Stick.

"Yes, yes, absolutely!" says Gretchen. She steps back and nudges Sam.

Stick's thoughts rush in, interrupting him. His elbow wobbles. He exhales and leans his head against the door.

"It's no good. I … can't do it," he says.

"Shh-shh-shh," says Gretchen. "Yes, you can. Concentrate now."

His elbow wobbles, ever so slightly. A single bead of sweat rolls down his face. And …

Click.

"Got it?" asks Gretchen.

"Got it," says Stick.

"Got it," says Sam as she passes Gretchen's phone back to her.

Gretchen steps into the science lab. Stick looks at Sam.

"What are you looking at?" she grunts. "*Jog on*."

Stick picks up his bag and runs.

BIG LITTLE LIES

Stick runs along the fence by the park, feeling the cold wind on his wet cheeks. He can hear the shouts of the football players on the pitches, but he doesn't look up to see if his friends are there. He thinks he hears someone shout his name, but he keeps running. He runs alongside the high wall and the memory of yesterday makes him sob again in big, noisy gulps. He runs alongside the row of witchy trees, their shadows blurring on the ground under his feet. By the time he gets to the canal he's out of breath. He drops his bag and leans his hands on the low wall of the bridge, looking down at his reflection in the dark water.

Two ducks peck at the slimy green weeds that trail from a shopping trolley in the canal. Buses grumble past on the road behind him, full of people on their way home from work and school. Stick picks up his bag and crosses the road that leads to Mum's work. Maybe he'll be in bed before she comes home. Then he won't have to tell her anything.

69

"Hey, little bro."

"Hey, Bella," says Stick.

Bella looks at Stick and screws up her face. "Where are your keys? Did something happen? Look at me." She holds him by the shoulders.

"Nothing happened," says Stick. "They're upstairs, I think."

"Hmmm," says Bella. Her phone pings and she smiles when she sees who the message is from. She shuts the door, still looking at the phone.

Stick dumps his bag in the hall and heads into the living room. "Hey, Dad."

"All right, lad?" says Dad. "Good day at the office?"

"Yeah, it was OK."

"See them new mates of yours?"

"No. Well, yes, just Milo. In science."

"Ah, that's good, lad. What's my old mate Bob teaching you? Still all apples falling from trees and the like?"

"That's more like primary school." Stick wonders what school must have been like for his dad. Everything in black and white, probably. "Who's Bob? Mr Jansari?"

"That's the man. Did a job with him a while back in Bigney."

Stick thinks about asking what it was, but his dad hasn't looked up from the HomeBot manual since he said hello. "What are you doing?" he asks instead.

"It says here that the HomeBot can talk to the fridge and the stereo, so I'm giving it a go."

"Did you get it working with the TV yet?" asks Stick.

"Not yet, lad, almost there."

Stick looks at the TV, where his dad has taped bits of

cardboard over the speakers.

"To keep the volume down," Dad says. "Just until I can figure this out."

Stick nods. "Did you have work today?"

Dad looks up from the manual, finally. "Not today, lad. Been waiting on a part for the van. Back tomorrow."

Stick isn't sure what his dad does for work. He doesn't work at all some days, and then other times he leaves before Stick and Bella get up for school and isn't back until they've gone to bed. Stick used to ask where he was going, but his dad would only answer by tapping his nose or saying silly things like, "To see a man about a dog," so he stopped asking.

"What did you cook?" he asks.

"Mushroom risotto. It's in the fridge, lad. Heat some up for yourself."

In two-and-a-half minutes...

While the risotto is warming up, Stick runs upstairs, uses the loo, washes his hands (of course), grabs a comic from his room and runs to get back downstairs again before the microwave pings.

"Yes!" he cries as he makes it back to the kitchen with one second to spare on the timer.

Dad calls from the other room. "Did you beat the clock?"

"Oh *yeah*!" calls Stick.

"Ace!" calls his dad.

They've played this game since Stick was old enough to run. One of his earliest memories is Dad counting down as Stick ran across the garden to him on his wobbly legs.

He grabs a fork and sits at the table with his comic and his dinner.

Stick shovels the risotto into his mouth as he turns the pages, getting lost in the story. By the time he gets to the cliffhanger, his belly is full and he's starting to feel a bit better.

"So…" he says, "can we watch TV?"

"We can," says Dad, "but I haven't been able to change the channel and the one it's on is mostly ads about that Mega Mall. Give it a go if you like."

Stick looks at the HomeBot. "Hey, HomeBot," he says. Nothing happens.

"It's 'Hey, Homie'," says Dad.

The HomeBot pings and its little lights flash. **"HEY, DAD!"** it says, and rolls over to Stick's dad.

"Oh yeah," says Stick. "Hey, Homie!"

"HEY, STICK!" says the HomeBot, and it spins round and rolls over to where Stick is sitting on the couch.

Stick looks at his dad. "How … how does it know my name?"

His dad shrugs. "Dunno, lad. AI maybe? I had to put in the details of the people in the house when I set it up. I suppose it worked out that you were the eleven-year-old boy by the sound of your voice."

"Okaaaaay… Does it have a camera?"

"Nope," says Dad, squinting at the manual. "Says here 'The HomeBot is equipped with an ultrasonic sensor and a microphone'. No camera. Don't think folk would want that."

"Then why," says Stick, "do I feel like it's watching me?"

The HomeBot blinks its little blue lights.

"It's the lights, lad," says Dad. "Installed like little eyes. Makes him look like a friendly little fella, I think. It connects to the Internet, you know. You can ask it anything."

Stick looks at the HomeBot. "OK. Hey, Homie," he says. "Are you watching me?"

"HEY, DAD!" says the HomeBot in a cheery mechanical voice. **"I am always listening, waiting for your command."**

"That doesn't really answer my question. What about – do you have a camera?"

The HomeBot is silent.

"You have to say 'Hey, Homie' every time," says Dad.

"OK," says Stick. "Hey, Homie, do you have a camera?"

"HEY, DAD!" says the HomeBot. **"I am equipped with an ultrasonic sensor and a microphone."**

"That doesn't really answer my question either," says Stick. "Hey, Homie, do you have a camera installed?"

"MY APOLOGIES, DAD!" says the HomeBot. **"I'm afraid I don't understand."**

"Do you have a camera inside you?"

"You have to say 'Hey, Homie'," says Dad.

"Oh, this is STUPID," says Stick, his voice rising.

The lights on the HomeBot blink, and it rolls slightly away from him.

"Whoa," says Dad, looking over at Stick. "Easy, lad. It's only a wee machine. Hey, what's up?" He gets up and sits next to Stick on the couch. "What's going on, kiddo?"

This is it. Stick can tell him everything and it will all be OK. His tears start to burn so he snuggles his head into his dad's chest and sniffs a bit. His dad's shirt smells of outside, of cold and engine oil and sawdust. He must've been doing something in the garden. Stick likes this smell.

"You know you can tell me anything, lad."

Stick tenses. He can feel a wave of sadness rolling over him, big and cold and grey. He keeps his face close to his dad's chest and the sad wave moves slowly through him. Stick can feel it tugging at the good things he's found in Little Town, trying to wash them away. Stick knows this sad wave. The feeling is strong, but it doesn't usually last. His dad says nothing. He keeps his arm round Stick and they sit. Just when Stick feels like he can't hold his breath any longer, his dad lets out a ferocious fart.

"*DAD!*" Stick laughs.

"What?" chuckles Dad. "Better out than in, lad! Anyway, it was that noisy, I doubt it was a stinker." He sniffs the air. "Oh! Beg your pardon! Must've been them lentils at lunchtime."

There's the sound of footsteps on the stairs and Bella puts her head round the door. "What are you two clowns giggling about?" Her expression changes quickly from a smile to a frown. "Ah jeez, who trumped?"

Stick and his dad both point at each other at the same time, which only makes them laugh harder. Bella manages to both roll her eyes and shake her head at the same time. "Honestly! What are you two like?" she asks, holding her nose as she turns and leaves.

"All right, kid?" Dad asks.

Stick nods and gives his dad a hug. He grabs his bag from the hall and heads up to his room.

8 · WHO LET THE DOGS OUT?

Mum is at the kitchen table, wearing her blue Supersavers Superdiscount Superstores uniform. "Hello, my handsome boy, what are you doing up this early?" she asks with a tired smile. "Come here to your old mum." She opens her arms, inviting Stick in for a hug. He sits on her lap and she gives him a big wet kiss on his cheek.

"Aw, Mum!" says Stick.

"What? I have to make the most of you while you're still little. Here, what's on your face? Have you been playing with Bella's make-up again?"

"What do you mean 'again'?" says Stick. "I did that when I was four! *Seven* years ago!"

Mum laughs. "All right, twiggy, no need to panic, I'm just winding you up." She smiles and looks closer. "Ah, I see. Someone fell asleep reading, did they?"

Stick nods and in his sleepy state he's not quick enough to stop Mum from wetting her thumb in her mouth and rubbing it on his cheek to get the ink off.

"Ew, gross!" says Stick, leaning away. "I'll wash it off when I have a shower."

Mum chuckles and gives a little sniff. "Not before time, I'd say. Up you pop, my little stinky. I'll make us some breakfast before I go to work."

"Didn't you have a late shift?" asks Stick. He fills the kettle at the sink. The blinds are open and the dawn sky is beginning to brighten into blue.

"Yes, love, but I'm on an early today. Listen to me, boring you about work! Pass me the eggs, will you? And tell me about school, stickle! How was day three?"

Stick hesitates. "It was … fine," he says.

"Just fine?" says Mum, cracking the eggs into the frying pan.

"Yeah, it was OK," says Stick.

"Hmm," says Mum, scrambling the eggs in the pan. "Put on the toast, will you? I suppose you had *such* a brilliant day on Tuesday, Wednesday was never going to be as good, was it?"

"Um … suppose you're right," says Stick, taking the butter out of the fridge.

"I'm really proud of you, pumpkin, you know that? So proud." She stops stirring the eggs to smile at him.

"Mum, the eggs!" says Stick.

"Oops," says Mum, scraping the eggs on to their plates. "Just in time! Get munching, munchkin." She chews thoughtfully, then swallows. "You know, I was thinking we should do something together, me and you."

"Like a spy mission?" says Stick, grinning.

Mum rolls her eyes. "No, you wally. Like a trip somewhere or an evening out. Cinema? What about tonight?"

Oops. Stick has forgotten to ask about the trip to the Mega Mall. "I can't tonight, Mum, I said I'd meet up with Ekam and Milo and Nic. We were going to meet in town, if that's OK? Sorry, I forgot to ask."

Mum beams. "You have plans? With friends?" She grabs him and pulls him into a massive hug, knocking over her tea and sending a fork clattering to the floor and bouncing off the HomeBot.

"Mum!" calls Stick. "You're squishing me!"

"Sorry!" says Mum, "I'm just so happy. Look at this mess. What am I like?" She glances at the clock. "I have to run!" She jumps up, plants a kiss on Stick's head, grabs her keys from the counter and heads for the door. "See you tonight, sausage! Have a great time in town! And we'll do something on Saturday, promise."

That's a yes, then. Stick grabs a cloth to mop up the tea. He picks up the fork from the floor and spots the HomeBot in the corner. Has it been in the kitchen all this time? He takes the dishes to the sink and washes up, then dries his hands. He sniffs an armpit. Hmm. Maybe a shower would be a good idea.

Back to school

Stick walks slowly to school. He's way too early, but he needed some time to think. He thinks about what happened at the lab. He thinks about what might happen next.

Possibility 1 – Gretchen was telling the truth. No more being picked on.

Possibility 2 – Gretchen was *not* telling the truth, and things will be just the same as before. Possibly more likely than Possibility 1.

Why did she want him to open the door anyway? His hands are cold and he puts them in his pockets. Yes, pockets.

He walks over the bridge by the canal, crossing the big road that goes to Mum's work. He passes the row of witchy trees, swaying gently in the breeze. He passes the high wall. He can almost hear the pounding of Sam's big boots again, getting louder as they get closer.

Wait a second. That *is* the pounding of Sam's big boots,

getting louder as they get closer!

Something's odd though. Sam's not shouting. Stick turns to see her legging it towards him. But … she doesn't look angry. She looks … *scared*?

And then he sees the dogs.

Teeth bared, tongues hanging out, drool dripping from their jaws as they gain on Sam. She gets close enough for Stick to see the fear in her eyes but she doesn't stop. He looks at the dogs, getting closer. Should he run too? They don't look *that* dangerous. Is that a cockapoo or a labradoodle?

Hmm. Stick puts a hand to his mouth and whistles.

The dogs fumble to a stop, bumbling into each other and looking around frantically, tongues flopping. They see Stick.

"Hey, doggies! Hey, hey!" says Stick.

"Get off! Ugh, stoppit!" says Stick, laughing.

"WINNIE! NOODLE! DOODLE! Come 'ere!"

The dogs abandon Stick and turn and run to the owner of the voice, who leans down to clip on their leads. When he stands up, he is the biggest man that Stick has even seen, and *old*. At least forty. He smiles, and Stick sees that two of his teeth are made of gold. Cool. He walks over to Stick.

"Sorry about that, kid," he says, rubbing his head. "They love chasing our neighbour."

He juts his chin in the direction of Sam.

"Sam?" says Stick.

"Yeah, that's the one. Heh." He laughs. "They're harmless, ain't they? But she always runs, so they always chase her. They like you though," he says, looking down. One of the dogs is licking Stick's leg. "Stop that, Noodle, leave the boy alone!" he says. "What's your name, son?"

"Stick," says Stick, looking up.

"Stick? Huh. Makes sense, I s'pose," he says. He puts out his massive hand for Stick to shake. "I'm Eric."

"Nice to meet you, Eric," says Stick.

"You too, Stick. See you around," says Eric. "Come on, you lot," he says to the dogs, and they trot obediently beside him as he heads back towards the canal.

Stick picks up his bag and walks over to Sam.

"All right?" he asks.

Sam nods. She's still out of breath.

"They're not going to hurt you, you know?" says Stick. "They just want to play."

Sam looks up at Stick. She nods, and in a quiet voice says, "Thanks."

Stick walks off, but Sam calls after him. "Hey, Stick!"

"Yeah?"

"Don't tell anyone about this."

Stick pauses.

"OK," he nods.

He turns, and carries on up the street.

Vox pops!

At lunchtime, Stick spots the boys in the canteen. He sits next to Ekam.

"All right, Stick?" says Ekam. "We missed you after school yesterday buddy, where were you?"

Stick tells them about the run-in with Gretchen and Sam at lunchtime, and about what happened at the science lab. When he's finished, the three boys stare at him.

"What?" says Stick.

"That's pretty serious," says Milo. "It's basically breaking and entering."

"Yeah," says Nic. "You probably shouldn't have done that."

"I know!" says Stick. He throws his hands up. "But what choice did I have? You don't understand! They were going to—"

"What?" asks Milo. "What were they going to do?"

86

"Nothing," says Stick. He looks down at the table.

"I get it," says Ekam. "Stick, mate. It's all right. You know if it gets too much, you can tell someone. Your mum and dad. Or a teacher."

Stick nods. "I know."

"And in other news, Gretchen is off sick today so at least you're not going to run in to her. And when Gretchen's away, Sam's... Well, she's..."

"What?" asks Stick.

"Different," says Nic, picking a chip off Stick's plate.

"Docile," says Milo.

"Docile? What does that mean?" asks Stick.

"Like a little lamb," says Nic, picking another chip off Stick's plate and using it to point across the canteen. "Observe, grasshopper."

"Vox pops," says Ekam. He shows Stick his badge. It's one of Sam's, only instead of "Bullied" it says "VoxPopped".

"Not sure that's a word," says Stick.

"No, not likely," says Ekam, "but it beats the alternative."

"Yes, I suppose it does," says Stick. He looks at his plate. He looks at Nic. "I'm sure I had more chips than that," he says.

"Really?" says Nic.

"Such a gannet," says Milo, grabbing Nic in a headlock. "Don't be eating the man's chips, can't you see he's hungry? You can get him some later."

"Later?" says Stick.

"At the mall?" says Milo. "Did you forget?"

"Oh yeah, I did forget!" says Stick. "Are we meeting there?"

"Get off!" says Nic, pushing Milo away. "Yeah. Me and Ekam have football training after last period." He looks at the others. "Five-ish?"

"Works for me!" says Ekam. "Gotta run, see you jokers later."

Milo looks at his timetable, then at Stick. "It appears, my friend, that we have an afternoon of running ahead. Oh joy. Did you bring your kit?"

Stick laughs. "I think I'll be OK without it."

Stick thought he was pretty awesome at running, but now he's not so sure. His legs hurt. His bum hurts. His everything hurts.

He thinks about the boy in that book he read, *Ghost*. He hopes they won't have sprint training again next time. Maybe it'll be table tennis. Or chess. Does chess count as PE? He looks over to Milo. "Is running meant to be torture?"

Milo chuckles. "Are you feeling the burn? Let's take a break."

"Those ads are *everywhere*," says Milo, looking across the road. "I saw one on a crisp packet yesterday. Ha – look!" He points at a bus with the same ad on the side. "I don't like those HomeBots. They're weird. Always listening."

"Me neither!" says Stick. "I swear my dad's follows me around."

"Ha!" says Milo. "Ours too! My dad was reading in the loo yesterday, and when he put down his newspaper it was sitting on the floor in front of him, blinking its evil little eyes. You should've heard him shouting. Blamed me, obviously, for putting it in there."

"Ha ha!" says Stick. "Did you?"

"No! Found its own way in. It follows us around like a creepy robot puppy. Don't know how it got up the stairs though. Hello, hello, what's all this?"

A massive limousine is cruising along the other side of the street.

"It's a massive limousine," says Stick with a grin.

"Very good, Mr Comedian."

The limousine glides to a stop outside Sew Special. The driver gets out, straightens her hat and moves to the other side to open the passenger door. A tall woman steps on to the pavement, dressed in a sharply cut mauve suit.

She folds her arms. She taps her foot. She looks very …
annoyed. She stares at someone inside the car.

"COME!" shrieks the woman.

"I don't want to—" the person inside says, but the
woman cuts her off.

"It's not about what you want though, is it, Gretchen?
Get out of the car THIS INSTANT!"

Gretchen? Isn't she supposed to be sick? The two boys
stare. They watch as the woman drags Gretchen out of
the car and into Sew Special. She makes her stand on a
stool in the window to be measured by a dressmaker who
looks about a hundred and fifty years old. Gretchen has
her arms crossed and is scowling like a walrus with wind.
The two boys chuckle.

"What a show!" says Milo. "Should've brought
popcorn."

"She looks livid!" says Stick.
"Ha! Serves her right."

So why doesn't he feel happy
about this? He looks at Milo.

"All right, dude?" asks Milo.

"C'mon," says Stick "I think
I've seen enough. Let's go."

MEGA MALL MATES

Stick hasn't been in the town square since the day they moved to Little Town. Dad went with the movers in the truck, and Mum followed in the van with Stick and Bella. The square looked really lovely then when they stopped for cake, lit up with strings of bulbs between the streetlights and in the trees around the fountain. He doesn't remember the Mega Mall being so big then, but now that he's standing in front of it he sees that it's absolutely, humungously massive – so tall that he can't even see the big satellite dish from the ground.

And boy is it *ugly*. It looks like it was put together from abandoned bits of schools that no one liked, stacked up and then stuck together with different coloured bricks. There are windows here and there and everywhere, all different shapes and sizes, and a big pipe snaking in and out of the walls – is it a … slide? High on top, above what looks like it might be a restaurant, tall and towering and already streaked with pigeon poo.

"Wow," says Milo. "What an absolute shambles. Is that Comic Sans?"

"Why does it look so awful? My eyes hurt," says Stick.

"Maybe they don't want people to hang around outside?" says Milo.

"Yeah," says Stick. "I feel a bit dizzy looking at it." He turns away, and spots Ekam and Nic heading their way. He nudges Milo. "Who's that with them?"

Milo squints. "Looks like Ekam's babysitting!"

"All right, boyos?" says Ekam. "Stick, this is my extremely annoying younger sister, Jasdeep. Don't believe anything she says."

Jasdeep puts out her hand. "Hi! I'm Jazz."

"Stick," says Stick. "Hi, Jazz. Nice to meet you."

Ekam looks up at the mall. "Some interesting architectural choices there. And by interesting I mean absolutely dreadful."

Nic arrives. "Heyheyhey, chummelinos! Wow," he says, looking up. "It's incredible! So cool. And a *slide*! Oh. M. Gosh. I *love* it. Let's go!"

CURIOUS

PROUD NERD

JAZZ

No sooner are they inside the Mega Mall than they lose their bearings. Every shop looks the same. There are only a few other shoppers, and everyone looks equally confused and totally lost.

"I'm hungry!" says Jazz.

"Then you should've eaten before we left," says Ekam.

"Ekam, you need to look after your little sister, man," says Milo with a wink at Stick.

Ekam shakes his head. He sighs. "Fine. There must be a food court somewhere, right?"

"Yeah," says Stick. "But there aren't any maps. Or signposts. Didn't we pass that Baron Ben's Butcher's already?"

"I think that was a Baron Ben's Baker's," says Nic. "This is totally hopeless. Is there anyone to ask?"

"We can ask a HomeBot!" says Jazz. "There, look!" She points at a huge screen in the window of Baron Ben's Bargain Binz, the biggest shop they've seen so far.

They go in. It's eerily quiet.

"Does anyone work here?" says Ekam.

Five HomeBots roll towards the gang, one stopping in

front of each of them.

"Welcome to Baron Ben's Bargain Binz! Please tell me how I may be of service!" they all say, but not quite at the same time. The kids look at each other.

"Where's the food court?" says Ekam.

"You have to say 'Hey, Homie' first," say Stick and Jazz together.

"Oh, for— Hey, Homie, where's the food court?" asks Nic.

The five HomeBots all answer at once, giving five different sets of directions that it takes the gang ten minutes to figure out and then another ten to follow. Eventually they find themselves in the food court.

"What's it going to be, gang?" says Milo, looking around. "Baron Ben's

SAY HEY HOMIE TO A HOMEBOT TODAY!

SAY HEY HOMIE TO A HOMEBOT TODAY!

TODAY!

Bargain Burgerz? Baron Ben's Tasty Treetz? Baron Ben's Mega Muffinz? Baron Ben's Super Spudz? A Perky Pretzel? A Cakey Cupcake? Yikes. Lots to choose from."

"Isn't it amazing?" says Nic. "So much choice. But I think," he says, "that today is a fries and milkshakes kind of day."

So, Stick...

Ten minutes later, the kids are sitting around in a booth in Baron Ben's Sippy Shakez. Stick has a chocolate and coconut milkshake with a raspberry swirl. It's quiet except for their slurping and crunching.

"So, Stick…" says Jazz.

"Here we go," says Milo.

"This should be good," says Nic.

"…can I ask you something?"

Stick stops mid-slurp. He looks up. He nods.

"Jazz…" says Ekam.

"It's all right," says Stick. "Go on."

"How does it work … when you have to go for a wee?"

"JAZZ!" says Ekam. "Seriously!" He puts his head in his hands.

"Knew it would be good," says Nic with a grin.

"Brilliant," says Milo. "Tip-flippin'-top."

"What do you mean?" says Stick.

"Well," says Jazz. "You don't have a…"

"What?" says Milo with a chuckle. "Willy?"

"Wally?" says Nic, chuckling as well.

"Johnson?" says Milo.

"John Thomas," says Nic.

"Tiddler!" says Milo.

"Tiddler?" says Ekam, looking up. "What? Who calls it that?"

"Widdler!" shouts Nic.

Milo laughs loudly, shooting strawberry milkshake out of his nose. Stick is laughing too. He slaps the table. "Piddler!"

"Piddler!" the boys echo back, laughing even more.

"Squiddler?" says Ekam, finally joining in.

Nic, Milo and Stick lean in, high-fiving him. Everyone is laughing now. Except Jazz. She sits with her arms folded. She raises an eyebrow. The left one.

"Morons."

"Oh my days and nights!" says Nic. "GREAT question, Jazz."

Stick is chuckling, breathless from laughing so much. "OK," he says. "I can answer. It's like … it's a bit like with the locker thing. When I concentrate really hard, or when I need it, parts of me change. So when I need to pee, it's there."

"Your squiddler, you mean?" says Milo.

"Jeez Louise," says Jazz, rolling her eyes. Suddenly her expression changes. "I have another question."

"Oh, what now?" says Ekam.

"Did those HomeBots follow us?"

The four boys turn and look. Five HomeBots are lined up outside the booth, silently blinking their little blue lights.

"Yikes," says Milo. "That's weird."

"Nah, they're probably just lost," says Nic. "Like everyone else in this place."

"I think they followed us," says Jazz.

"Why would they do that?" says Nic. "That's *ridiculous*."

"Because they're spying on us," says Jazz. "Because they're spying on everyone."

Nic laughs. "That's total nonsense!"

"I don't know," says Milo. "I told you what happened to my dad in the loo."

"Your dad? He probably fell asleep on the toilet again and dreamed it," says Nic.

"What about Mrs Taylor in number forty-eight?" says Jazz, looking at Ekam. "She told Mum that her HomeBot follows her around the flat. Says it appears every time she opens a cupboard or the fridge. Like it wants to look inside. Or my mate Jessica. Says her mum put hers on the kitchen counter last week when she was cleaning the floor and it pushed the kettle off and smashed it."

"What did she do?" asks Milo.

"Went out and bought a new kettle, didn't she? They're always drinking tea round hers."

"Mrs Taylor says her cat can count to sixty," says Ekam. "So she's not the world's most reliable witness. That kettle thing is weird though."

"I don't buy it," says Nic.

"Ours is a bit creepy," says Stick, slurping the last of his milkshake. "I feel like it's always there, listening to me."

"Ours too," says Jazz, nodding.

"Ooooooooh!" says Nic in a mocking voice. "Maybe they're listening now! Shhh, don't let them know you're on to them! Hey, robots! Are you all listening? Are you watching us?"

The row of HomeBots doesn't move, but their little blue lights all blink together, once.

"You didn't say 'Hey, Homie'," says Jazz.

"Whatever," says Nic. "This is dumb. The robots are *not* watching us. I'm so over this. Let's bounce, I need to get my bus anyway."

"Did you want to check out the satellite dish, Stick?" asks Milo.

"Nah, it's OK," says Stick. "It's already late, I'll see it some other time."

The others nod. They pick up their trays and head towards the bins, stepping over the row of HomeBots.

"Bye, HomeBots!" calls Nic. "See you soon!"

Jazz shakes her head. Milo looks at Stick and shrugs.

Most of the other customers have already left when the gang gets back to where the shops are. "OK, pals," says Ekam, "Any guesses as to the way out?"

"This way," says Nic, confidently marching ahead.

Within a minute, they're lost again. Milo suggests going back to the food court and retracing their steps instead of going further but they can't find their way back there either. They turn a corner and they're in a massive atrium, looking at a huge stage with another gigantic screen showing the same Jonny Vidwire ad, this one even bigger than the one outside.

"Must be for the concert," says Ekam.

"Where your *girlfriend* might be performing!" says Milo, elbowing him. "Hi, everyone, I'm Alannah!" he says in a high-pitched voice, miming a microphone and patting his hair. "And I'd like to dedicate this song to my *one*, my true love – Ekam Alexander Patrick Aloysius

Ebeneezer Singh, without whom I wouldn't have found the strength, the courage—"

"All right, enough," says Ekam, laughing. "Ebeneezer? Where did you get that?"

"Dunno," says Milo. "I think I've been stuck in this mall for too long. Which way next?"

"There's an exit here," calls Jazz from behind the stage, "but it's locked."

The boys look at Stick. Stick smiles.

Two minutes later, they're in an alleyway outside the mall. They can see the lights of the town square in the distance.

"That was so *cool*," says Jazz as they walk towards the square.

"Thanks," says Stick. He feels a little wobbly. Unlocking the door brought back memories of the day before, and with them the dark, heavy swirls.

"You all right?" asks Ekam.

"Yeah, I'm OK," says Stick. "Thanks. I'm going to get a bus home, I think."

The kids walk to the town square and say their goodbyes. Behind them, the lights in the mall go out, one by one.

FINALLY FRIDAY

It's Friday, and Stick is arriving at school. He's in a good mood. Why? Mum's given him permission to stay late for the Friday Factor final, which he's excited about. AND he's looking forward to hanging out with his friends again. Maybe Gretchen and Sam will even keep their end of the deal...

He picks up his books from his locker and files into assembly with the rest of the Year Sevens. He spots Milo and Ekam, who have saved him a seat.

"All right, Stick?" says Ekam. "Have a good wee this morning?"

The three boys laugh.

"That was too funny last night," says Milo. "What is your sister like?"

"Like a nosey nine-year-old," says Ekam. "I can't take her anywhere. Hello, O'Leary's not looking too chirpy this morning. What's up with her? Which one of you lot's been singing out of tune?"

Miss O'Leary is storming on to the stage, and not in an about-to-launch-into-song way, more in an about-to-launch-a-misbehaving-student-into-orbit way. She reaches the podium and grabs the mic.

"SILENCE!" she spits, sprinkling saliva on the front row.

Uh-oh.

An immediate hush falls. It's quiet enough to hear a mouse trump. Miss O'Leary glares at the silenced students. The kids in the front row lean back in their chairs.

"Good," she says in a low voice, sounding somehow both disappointed and angry. "I have to tell you," she growls, "I am disappointed. And I am angry."

"Today," she says, gripping the sides of the podium and looking off to the right. "Today was to be a JOYOUS day. One filled WITH *song* and *laughter* and the THRILL of competition and school spirit and INSTEAD it has been tainted – TAINTED – by the actions of one of you. Spoiled. Everything SPOILED!"

She throws back her head and sighs, one hand pressed against her forehead in anguish.

Quite dramatic.

The randomly shouted words are making the kids in the front row jump, and several are gripping the sides of their chairs. She continues, "Today was to be my – our wonderful day with Jonny Vidwire HIMSELF but instead –" she pauses. Is that a tear? – "INSTEAD I must deal with the fact that one of you BROKE INTO the science lab on Wednesday after school and STOLE Mr Jansari's laptop."

There's a huge gasp from the assembled children, followed by furious whispering. Ekam and Milo turn to Stick.

"You didn't say anything about a laptop!" hisses Ekam. "What the…?"

"Dude," says Milo with a quiet glare. "You didn't. Tell me you didn't."

"NO!" Stick whispers back, a bit too loudly. "I don't know anything about a laptop!"

Oh no. This is bad, Stick. This is very bad.

And here come the swirls, heavy and dark.

"SILENCE! SILENCE!" shrieks Miss O'Leary,

thumping the podium with her fist. "Quit your chatter. I will be making enquiries throughout the school today, but if ANY of you have any information I urge you to come forward. Until this matter is resolved, consider tonight's Friday Factor final CANCELLED. Now go to class."

The kids howl in protest. A boy and a girl near Alannah burst into tears. Miss O'Leary stays at the podium as the kids stand and protest. No mic drop. No cool exit.

Nic joins the boys as they make their way out.

"Stick…" he begins.

"It wasn't me," hisses Stick. "I don't know anything about this."

"You have to tell O'Leary what happened, Stick," says Ekam. "It must have been Gretchen and Sam. What about everyone who's looking forward to tonight?"

"What about Alannah, you mean?" snaps Stick. "I'm not saying anything. They'll only make it worse. You don't get it. None of you get it." He can feel the burning behind his eyes again but he won't give in to it, not now. "I'm going to class." He storms off.

The boys watch him go, but don't say anything.

Solo Stick...

Stick pushes through the crowd until he finds a quiet corridor. His heart is thumping. Why is everything so difficult? Why can't anything go right?

Breathe, Stick.

He stops and pulls out his timetable. Oh, that's just great. ICT with Birdy. Just when things can't get any worse. And he's late, of course, so he picks up his bag and runs. He turns a corner to see Gretchen and Sam leaning on some lockers. They're not doing anything in particular, just hanging around looking mean. Stick doesn't stop. As he runs past, Gretchen catches his eye. She winks, raises a finger to her lips and whispers, "Shhhh!"

Stick runs round the corner, past the main entrance and down to the computer lab. He makes it to his seat just before Miss Bird arrives. He looks out of the window, at the light through the frosted glass. There are no crows today. Why did he snap at Ekam? Miss Bird drops her handbag and phone on her desk and looks at the class.

"Good morning, class."

"Good morning, Miss Bird."

"So," she says, sitting on the edge of her desk. She reaches into her bag and takes out a nail file. She begins to file her nails, already as pointed as talons.

"It appears we have a thief in our midst. A *sticky-*fingered student among you."

Stick looks up. She's looking directly at him, a sneer curling on her lips.

What's going on? *Does she know?*

"Still, I do hope we'll find out who the culprit is before the end of the day. It would be *ever* so disappointing if we were all to miss the Friday Factor final because of one selfish student. One. Little. Criminal." She sucks her teeth, still looking at Stick. "Tsk. Well. Back to work, everyone! Where did we get to on Tuesday? Ah yes, VPNs."

Stick looks around. Everyone is busy logging in to their consoles except for Alannah, who is staring at him.

"What's going on?" she mouths silently.

Stick raises his eyebrows and shrugs.

Alannah turns back to her console and Stick turns back to his worries. He just needs to get through today. It's going to be OK. He didn't take the laptop. He wasn't even in the science lab with Gretchen and Sam. It's going to be OK.

Isn't it?

THE PROOF

After class, Stick makes a hasty exit to avoid Alannah's questions. He finds his way to maths and makes it on time, for a change. He sits quietly through a lesson on trigonometry, worrying about everything. Should he tell Miss O'Leary? Or will that make things worse? The more he thinks about everything, the heavier the dark, heavy, swirling feelings grow.

At break he heads towards the canteen but when he sees Nic, Ekam and Milo by the door he changes his mind. He turns to go somewhere else but sees Gretchen and Sam at the other end of the corridor, picking on someone. This is impossible! He drops his bag by the nearest lockers and slips behind them.

Who keeps throwing their manky sandwiches here? Grim. Still, at least he doesn't have to talk to anyone. He waits, standing in the dust. He hears students chatting to each other as they walk past, complaining about the cancellation of the Friday Factor final and making guesses about who could have stolen the laptop.

Stick stands there and thinks and thinks. What if

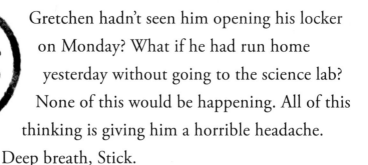

Gretchen hadn't seen him opening his locker on Monday? What if he had run home yesterday without going to the science lab? None of this would be happening. All of this thinking is giving him a horrible headache.

Deep breath, Stick.

He waits until the bell rings and then waits a bit longer, until he can't hear any voices. He slips out from behind the lockers, grabs his bag and legs it to science.

Milo is already at the desk when he gets there. "All right?" he asks. "Missed you at break, dude."

Stick nods. "Yeah, I was…"

"Not in the mood for people? That's all right." Milo lowers his voice. "You need time to think. You know, for what's it's worth—"

"I know," says Stick. "I should go to the head."

"Yeah, that too, but I was gonna say that if Gretchen and Sam did take the laptop then I reckon they'll happily let you take the blame."

"I know, but—" Stick stops.

Mr Jansari has arrived. Everyone looks at the teacher. He clears his throat.

"Right, now," he says. "Listen up, Year Seven, you've all heard what happened after school on Wednesday. Needless to say, I'm not happy." He looks around. "I hope it wasn't any of you, future scientists." He sighs. "We're here to learn, so let's concentrate on that and pick up where we left off. Tangential velocity. Milo, can you give us a quick summary?"

Stick keeps his head down for the rest of the class, and all through geography as well. He keeps his head down on the way to the canteen, he keeps his head down as he takes his tray to sit on his own, far from the queue and the busy tables. He keeps his head down as he eats. He hears some commotion at one of the tables in the middle, but he keeps his head down still. Maybe he can just sit here until the bell rings. Maybe no one has to know. Maybe Gretchen and Sam will be caught, and the Friday Factor final will go ahead, and no one will find out that it was him who opened the science lab door. Maybe everything will be OK.

Why is it so quiet?

Stick looks up.

Everyone is looking at him.

Gretchen steps forward.

"YOU!" she shrieks. "It was YOU!" She's holding her phone high above her head, and on it is a video of Stick at the door of the science lab. "LOOK!" she shrieks again.

"Two thousand and four views," says Miss O'Leary. "Not *quite* viral, is it?"

"No, miss," says Stick.

"Not that I want my students here to be the stars of any viral videos, of course."

"No, miss."

"Nor of any videos where they are breaking into school property. *Breaking the law, even.*"

Gulp.

LIVE, LAUGH, LOVE!

MISS O'LEARY: IN A CLASS OF HER OWN!

TEACHER BY DAY, SINGER BY NIGHT!

"No, miss." Stick is staring at the floor. The carpet is particularly ugly.

"Look up. Do you have anything to say for yourself?"

He looks up. "No, miss."

Miss O'Leary sighs. "Stick. I know that it must have been difficult for you to start school here in the middle of the year, and ordinarily I would be prepared to make allowances for someone in your position."

Stick looks up, hopeful.

"However, breaking and entering, and theft, I cannot sanction."

"But, miss, I didn't steal the laptop!"

"No? Did you just open the door of the lab for fun? A little jape?"

"No, I…"

Mr Jansari coughs. "We found these in the lab, Stick." He holds out Stick's dice, yellow with black dots. "In the drawer where I keep my laptop. They have your name on them. Do you want to tell me how they got there?"

"I…" Stick begins. He wants to say, *I can explain*, but he can't. Not without saying that Gretchen and Sam were there, and that they forced him to open the door. And then what?

"Yes, Stick? Do please explain yourself. I'm waiting."

There's a knock at the door. Miss O'Leary ignores it. She stares at Stick. There's another knock, louder. Miss O'Leary looks up, irritated.

"COME!"

The door opens and Miss Bird pokes her nose around it.

"Yes, Miss Bird, is it urgent?"

Miss Bird smiles. Stick hasn't seen her smile before. It looks … fake?

"Yes, Miss O'Leary, it's about Bob's laptop."

"We were just discussing that with Stick here. What is it?"

"I've found it."

"What do you mean, you've found it?"

"I've found it," she says, passing the laptop to Mr Jansari. "It was in the staffroom. On top of the fridge."

"On top of the fridge?"

"Yes, Miss O'Leary. Next to the biscuits." She looks at Mr Jansari. "You must have left it there and forgotten about it, silly. What are you like?" she asks, rolling her eyes.

Mr Jansari looks at the laptop, and then at Miss Bird. He looks sceptical. "But—" he begins, but Miss Bird interrupts him.

"Don't mention it!" she chirps.

Miss O'Leary seems flustered. "Yes, well, thank you, Miss Bird."

"No problem," replies Miss Bird in a strange, sweet tone. But as she leaves, she gives Stick a cold look. "See you in class, Stick."

Miss O'Leary presses the button on the intercom and coughs into the mic. "ATTENTION, EVERYONE! WONDERFUL news! Mr Jansari's laptop has been found. The Friday Factor final will GO AHEAD as planned this afternoon. That is all."

Stick hears the sudden roar of students cheering all over the school. He's not feeling very cheery.

Miss O'Leary claps her hands. "Well. Good. But what am I to do with you, Stick? It appears that you did not take the laptop, and yet –" she glances at the laptop screen – "you clearly broke into the lab." She drums on the desk with her fingertips, considering. "I think …

no Friday Factor final with Jonny Vidwire for you, and detention all of next week with Miss Bird. Lunchtime *and* after school."

Stick nods.

"Mr Jansari?"

Mr Jansari is still staring at his laptop and appears deep in thought.

"BOB?"

"Yes," says Mr Jansari, looking up. He nods. "Right. Seems appropriate." He turns to Stick. "We've tried to call your parents, but we haven't been able to get through."

"They're at work, sir."

Miss O'Leary nods. "Very well. When you get home, you can let them know what you've done, if they haven't already seen it online. Off you go."

Stick nods. "Yes, miss."

When Stick gets home, Mum is at the table on her laptop again. She looks up when he comes in and sees right away that something's up.

"All right, poppet? I thought you were going to the Friday thing with your friends? I had a missed call from school too – what's happened?"

Stick looks at his mum. He feels a lump in his throat and he's afraid that if he opens his mouth to answer, all that will come is tears.

Mum closes the laptop and reaches her arms out to him. "Come, twiglet. Come here."

And Stick does. She scoops him up in her arms and puts him on her lap. She puts her arms around him and squeezes him tight. Mum holds him as he sobs, stroking his head and rocking him in her arms. "All right, sweet pea, let it out. Good boy."

"I'm sorry, Mum," Stick cries, his face muffled in her jumper.

"It's OK, chicken. Good thing my uniform already needs a wash, eh?"

Stick laughs then, through the snotty tears, and Mum smiles. Stick lifts his head from her shoulder and looks at her.

"I did something bad, Mum," he says. "And I lied."

She looks at him and strokes his face, wiping his smudgy tears.

Dad appears at the door. "Everything OK, lad?"

Mum catches Dad's eye. "Put the kettle on, will you, love?" She turns back to Stick. "Whatever it is, Stick, I'm sure it's not the end of the world. Tell us what happened."

So he does. He tells them about Gretchen and Sam throwing away his things and about how he opened his locker. He sits at the table with his cup of tea, and Mum and Dad sit with him and listen quietly. The more Stick tells them, the less he cries. The dark, heavy swirls in his belly don't go away, but they start to feel a bit lighter. When he gets to the part about the science lab, he shows them the clip on Mum's laptop. The three of them watch silently; the only other sound in the kitchen is the HomeBot bumping into cupboards. When the clip ends, Mum and Dad look at each other. Dad is first to speak.

"Well, lad. I am impressed, but that's, er…"

"*Illegal?*" suggests Mum. "Stick, why didn't you tell us about these girls straight away? You know you can tell us anything."

Stick feels the lump in his throat growing again. He sobs. "Because I knew you'd be disappointed and we'd have to move again and then it will just happen again—"

Dad and Mum both reach over and hug Stick at the same time.

"It's OK, it's OK," says Dad. "You didn't let anything happen. It's not your fault."

"Dad's right," says Mum. "None of this is your fault. And no one is moving. We're very proud of you, you know that?"

"Ymmm fwwfffn mm," says Stick.

"What's that, poppet?" says Mum.

Stick wriggles out from between their arms and looks at both of them. "I said, you're squishing me!"

"But that's only because you're so squishable, my little darling!"

"Mum, you're so soppy! Stop it," says Stick.

"She's right, lad, you are a bit," says Dad, grabbing him again in a big hug and rubbing his head. "And we are proud of you. Look at you, making new friends in your first week." The mention of his friends reminds Stick that he snapped at Ekam, and he tries to hide this new worry as Dad carries on. "It's OK, Stick. We know it ain't exactly easy for you, son, and here you are making a real good go of it. We all make mistakes, and that's OK." He stands Stick on the floor and looks at him. "All right?"

Stick wipes his nose and manages a small smile. "All right," he says.

"We'll need to talk to Miss O'Leary on Monday, Stick, you know?" says Mum. "And I think it's fair to say that while you have detention, you're grounded, so make the most of your freedom this weekend."

Stick nods.

"What do you want her to do about Sam and Gretchen? About the bullying?"

"I … I don't know yet," says Stick. "Can I have a think about it?"

"Of course, love. Whatever you decide to do, we will support you, OK?" says Mum.

"OK," says Stick.

Security measures

Half an hour later, Stick, Mum and Dad are sitting in the living room with their dinner. Stick takes a big bite of his fish-finger sandwich and munches happily. He feels tired, but it's a good kind of tired.

The massive TV is gone and in its place is their normal-sized old one.

"So," says Stick, "what happened to the TV?"

"Your dad made the very sensible decision to take it back and get a refund. Isn't that right, Simon?"

"Yup," says Dad. "They let me keep the HomeBot though."

"And where's Bella?" he asks, through a mouth full of lettuce and mayo. "Did you take her back for a refund too?"

"Nice," says Dad, leaning over to high-five Stick.

"Chew first, chat second, Stick," says Mum. "She's out with one of the girls from sixth form. Gone to the square, I think. Oh, how was the mall last night?"

Stick swallows. "Good. A bit weird. Some HomeBots followed us."

Mum and Dad look at each other.

"What do you mean?" says Dad.

"Well, we asked for directions and then we were having shakes and fries, and talking about the HomeBots breaking stuff in people's houses, and we looked around and they were just there, lined up next to us."

"Then what happened?"

"Nothing," he shrugs. "We left and the HomeBots stayed in the shakes place." He looks around. "Where's ours, anyway?"

As if on cue, the HomeBot rolls into the living room.

"Here it is," says Dad.

"Yeah," says Stick. "We think they're breaking things all over town so everyone will have to buy more stuff from Baron Ben."

Mum and Dad look at each other again. "That's quite a theory, Stick," says Mum. "Although this one does spend a lot of time bashing into our cupboards."

The three of them look at it. "Do you think it's listening now?" asks Stick.

"We could just switch it off," says Mum.

"Doesn't have an off button," says Dad, "but I have figured out how to enable some privacy settings. Watch. Hey, Homie…"

The HomeBot blinks its little eyes and rolls over to Dad.

"HEY, DAD!" it says, in its way-too-chirpy voice.

Dad reaches down beside the couch and picks up a red bucket. He places it over the HomeBot.

Mum and Stick laugh.

"Simon, you're such an idiot," says Mum. "It can still hear us, you know."

"Brilliant," says Stick. The HomeBot starts to move, pushing the bucket around the carpet. "We could draw a face on it."

"I was thinking that," says Dad. "Maybe some googly eyes?"

"Did you ever get it to talk to the fridge?" asks Stick.

"No, lad, I gave up in the end. Life's too short. It didn't really follow my instructions anyway – it ignored me for hours last night, wouldn't respond at all. Still, it does have some uses." He leans over and puts his empty plate on top of the upturned bucket. "Hey, Homie, go to the kitchen."

"YES, DAD!" says the HomeBot, and off it goes.

Mum rolls her eyes.

"Shall we see if there's a movie on?" asks Dad, picking up the remote.

13 A STRANGE SATURDAY

It's already light when Stick wakes up on Saturday. The house is quiet. He doesn't remember getting to bed. Maybe he fell asleep during the movie and Dad brought him upstairs? Stick gets up, opens the curtains and looks out over the estate. The van is gone so Dad must be at work. He hears Bella's laughing voice through the wall. She's on the phone to someone. What time is it?

He plods downstairs to the kitchen, spotting the HomeBot in the living room as he walks past. When he opens the fridge it's already next to him, lights blinking.

"Get lost," he tells it.

He sits at the table with his comic and a bowl of Supersavers Supercrunchy Choco Nut Pops. The HomeBot rolls around the floor, bumping into things, but it doesn't leave the room.

He hears Bella thumping down the stairs. She puts her head round the door. "Afternoon, doofus!"

"Hey, Bella, what's going on?"

"Apparently you are, little badman. Mum says you're a VidWire star now. Exciting!"

"I—" says Stick, but Bella interrupts.

"Details later! Gotta run, I'm late – see ya!" She disappears, slamming the front door behind her.

Stick looks at the HomeBot. "What just happened?"

"WASN'T SHE TALKING ABOUT YOUR LITTLE BREAK-IN, STICKY?"

What the…? What kind of question is that?

"But I didn't say 'Hey, Homie'," says Stick.

The HomeBot rolls over and bumps into his chair.

"YES, STICK?"

"Have you been eavesdropping?" asks Stick.

No response.

"Hey, Homie, have you been listening?"

"I'M SORRY, I'M AFRAID I DON'T KNOW HOW TO ANSWER THAT QUESTION," says the HomeBot.

"That's convenient," says Stick.

"YES," says the HomeBot.

OK, *what* is going on?

Stick looks around. Dad's security bucket is on the coffee table. He gets it and drops it on top of the HomeBot.

"That's better," he says.

What now? He needs to tell someone about this. What time did Ekam say they play football in the park?

Always Say Hey, Homie!

It's super busy at the park. The sun's out, and mums and dads have dragged their screaming kids into the fresh air, away from their TVs and GameBoxes. Dogs and seagulls are fighting noisily over crisp packets and empty takeaway cartons and an old man is feeding the ducks, singing to himself. Two teenagers roller-skate arm in arm past Stick, whistling as they go.

Over the racket, Stick hears the thump of a football being kicked and the shouts of players and he cycles towards the noise. As he gets closer, he spots Ekam. He drops his bike on the ground next to some others and waits until Ekam sees him. When he does, Stick raises one arm in a kind of half wave. Ekam nods, but he doesn't come over. So Stick waits.

What if Ekam is angry? What if he's *really* angry? What if he doesn't want to be friends any more? He feels a swirl in his belly…

Easy, Stick. Let's wait and see, shall we?

The game carries on, and Stick watches one of the bigger players boot the ball hard and low past the goalie. As he celebrates, the ball bounces off a park bench and ricochets into the slimy pond.

"Nice one, Nigel!" calls one of the other players.

"Yeah, well done, Nige. Skills, mate," shouts another.

Stick chuckles.

Ekam looks around and jogs over to Stick.

"All right, Ekam?" says Stick, hopefully. Ekam nods. "I … I'm sorry about yesterday."

Ekam doesn't say anything. He raises one eyebrow. The left one.

Stick continues. "I shouldn't have snapped at you. You were right. You were all right."

Ekam nods. "Yep."

"I told Mum and Dad everything last night. I should have told them sooner."

Ekams nods again. "Good."

Stick takes a breath. "I'm sorry about what I said about Alannah."

"That's OK. I actually was thinking about her when I said what I said."

"OK," says Stick, nodding. "So … did she win?"

"Ha!" Ekam laughs. "No, she did not," he says, picking up his bike from the pile. "You'll never guess what the winning song was about!"

"What?" says Stick, grabbing his bike.

"What's weird and creepy and always annoying?"

Stick thinks. "Birdy?"

"Guess again. Something that's everywhere."

"Jonny Vidwire?"

"Oooh, getting warmer. Like Jonny, but creepier."

A lot has happened this week, but the creepiest thing was *having a conversation with the HomeBot this morning.*

"Um … our creepy HomeBot?"

"BINGO!" shouts Ekam. "Some random Year Eights singing A SONG about flipping HOMEBOTS win a competition sponsored by THE GUY WHO MAKES THE HOMEBOTS!"

"Whoa!" says Stick. "I see you have strong feelings about this turn of events."

"I do. It *stinks*. What a swizz."

"Swizz?" says Stick.

"Like a fix," says Ekam. "An inside job. A fraud. A sham. And do you know what the worst thing is?"

"No—" starts Stick, but Ekam interrupts.

"The song is GREAT! It's RIDICULOUSLY FLIPPIN' CATCHY! Listen."

"I'm not sure I want to," says Stick.

"NO CHOICE!" says Ekam. "Consider it payback for yesterday. Ready?"

"No," says Stick, sticking his fingers in his ears.

Ekam starts to sing.

> Homie-homie
> HooooooomeBot,
> I love my HomeBot!
> Always by my side-bot,
> Wherever I may roam-bot.
> Homie-homie-HomeBot
> I love myyyyyyyyy
> HomeBot!

That. Is. Dreadful.

But Ekam's right. It *is* catchy.

Wait – is this what the roller-skaters were whistling? What was that old man singing to the ducks?

"Is that it?" asks Stick.

"Yep," says Ekam. "That's it. Repeated about eighteen times. Then at the end they did this awful cheerleading thing where they jumped around and clapped and said *'Always! Say! Hey! Homie!'*. It's already got ten million views on VidWire."

"Since yesterday?" says Stick. "How is that even possible?"

"Dunno," shrugs Ekam. "It makes you yesterday's news though, my lock-picking friend. No one's clicking on the clip of your little misdemeanour any more. How did it go with O'Leary anyway?"

As they push their bikes out of the park, Stick tells him about Miss Bird showing up with the laptop when he was in the head's office.

"So it was in the staffroom all along? That doesn't make any sense," says Ekam. "There's something fishy going on here. Why did Gretchen make you open the door of the lab then?"

"Maybe she stole something else?"

"Nah, we'd know about it by now," says Ekam. "She loves bragging."

"What are you thinking?" asks Stick.

"I'm thinking," says Ekam, "that Gretchen took the laptop and that Birdy's *lying*. How could Jansari not notice he'd left it in the staffroom? On top of the fridge, *next to the biscuits?* Come on! Teachers love biscuits! Mr Bell is about twenty-eight per cent Jammie Dodger. Somebody else would've seen the laptop there before Birdy did."

"OK," says Stick, nodding. "So where did she get it then? From Gretchen?"

"No idea," says Ekam. They walk past two girls

swinging a skipping rope between them, singing the HomeBot song as a boy jumps. "Everyone is singing that song! It's so strange."

"Speaking of strange…" says Stick. He tells Ekam about the HomeBot talking to him in the kitchen. Ekam nods as he listens. He looks at Stick.

"Ours was acting weird this morning too," he says. "It asked Mum if she was 'sure about that top' when she came into the kitchen and then it said she should go to the mall."

"That's bizarre!" says Stick.

"You didn't see the top she was wearing," says Ekam.

"But how did *it* see it? They don't have cameras," says Stick. He frowns, and he thinks.

"Maybe it's just programmed to ask. What's up?" asks Ekam, noticing Stick's expression.

"There's a serious amount of odd stuff going on. The HomeBots following us at the mall and acting weird everywhere, the missing-not-missing laptop, the winning song going viral in like five minutes. Everything. Is it always like this in Little Town?"

"Um, not usually," says Ekam. "It's definitely been stranger since everyone got a HomeBot that's been programmed to break stuff so Gretchen's dad can make more money. We think. Allegedly," says Ekam.

"Gretchen's dad…" says Stick, scratching his chin as they walk. He turns to Ekam. "Let's try to figure this out."

They lean their bikes against a bench by the canal and sit. A man walks past, humming to himself as he pushes a baby in a buggy. Ekam recognizes the HomeBot tune and shakes his head.

"OK," says Stick. "What do we *actually* know?"

"One," says Ekam, "we know that Gretchen and Sam were in the lab on Wednesday. Because you very kindly let them in."

"Thanks for the reminder," says Stick. "Two: we know that Jansari's laptop which was *probably* in the lab went missing, also on Wednesday," says Stick.

"Because Gretchen *probably* nicked it. Three: the laptop showed up again on Friday, with Birdy," says Ekam. "So where was it in between?"

"At Gretchen's house maybe? She wasn't at school on Thursday," says Stick. "But why would she take it home? She could have got caught with it … unless … unless she was *meant* to take it home?"

"What do you mean?" asks Ekam.

"I mean, the Baron – could he have made Gretchen steal it?" says Stick.

"That's a horrible idea. Why? What's on the laptop that he wants?"

"I dunno. Super-secret spy stuff?"

"Do you read a lot of comics?"

Stick nods. "Super Boy mostly."

"Correct answer! Me too," says Ekam. "OK, OK, so let's say that Mr Jansari is a spy…"

"It's totally possible," says Stick. "He is super smart."

Ekam nods. "And why would he be spying on the Baron?"

"Because he noticed all the same weird HomeBot stuff we did?"

"OK … and he did call the Baron a megalomaniac."

"It *kinda* works," says Stick. "But it doesn't explain how Birdy got the laptop. I don't know. Something doesn't add up. I feel like I'm forgetting something…"

"What we need," says Ekam, interrupting his thoughts, "is more information. We need evidence. Come on, let's go." He hops on his bike and starts cycling towards the canal.

"Wait, what? Wait up! Where are we going?" calls Stick.

14 TROUBLE AT THE MANSION

By the time Stick catches up with Ekam, they're already at the edge of town, out past the mosque and the go-kart track.

"Slow down!" shouts Stick. "Where are we going?"

Ekam skids to a stop and grins. "Come on, slowcoach!" He waits for Stick to catch up. "That," he says, pointing up a hill, "is where we're going. Baron Ben's mega mansion. If we're going to find anything, we'll find it there."

Stick groans. "Why is everything at the top of a hill?"

"It's all downhill on the way back, buddy. *Chop chop*."

"Oh, ha ha," says Stick.

They start to cycle up the hill and it takes roughly forever to reach the mega mansion.

"What do you think—" starts Stick, but he's interrupted by the barking of a huge slobbering hound that's hurling itself against the other side of the gate.

"I think that we should move away from the murderous attack dog," says Ekam, "and try to find another way in. Come on."

They continue up the hill, but there aren't any more gaps in the wall. There are some woods on the other side of the road though. Stick looks up at the bare branches of the trees.

"Hey, Ekam," he calls. "We could climb up to look?"

"Worth a try," says Ekam.

They wheel their bikes into the woods and find a tree that looks tall enough. Stick shimmies up it in no time and calls down to Ekam. "Come on, slowcoach!"

"Yeah, all right," says Ekam. "Coming." He gets to the top and wriggles around to wedge himself between some branches. The boys look out. They can see across the road and into the walled grounds of the mansion. This is what they see:

Truck with HomeBot ad on the side

Six-car garage

Classy stretch limo

Twelve-bedroom mansion

Ravens

Gigantic satellite dish

Howling dogs

Big cats

"Classy," says Stick.

"All very tasteful," says Ekam. "Hello, who's this?"

They watch as a car moves slowly up the driveway towards the house.

"I've seen that car near school," says Ekam.

The car has stopped and the driver is making their way quickly to a door at the side of the garage. It's Miss Bird.

"What's *she* doing here?" asks Stick.

"Dunno," says Ekam. "Let's wait and see."

They don't have to wait long. Within moments they hear shouting coming from inside. They can't make out what's being said, but suddenly the door bursts open and Gretchen storms out, followed by a furious-looking Miss Bird.

Miss Bird starts shouting at Gretchen and she starts to shout back, which gets the dogs barking, which gets the cats howling, which gets the ravens screeching. The boys look at each other and shrug. They can't make out a word over the noise. A window in the mansion opens and a very red-faced man leans out and roars at both of them.

"SHUT UP!" It's the Baron.

Gretchen, Miss Bird, the dogs, the cats and the ravens all go quiet. The Baron goes back inside and in a few seconds reappears downstairs at the front door with Gretchen's mum. Stick and Ekam stare. They've only ever seen the Baron on TV before and he looks much smaller in real life. And much redder. Gretchen and Miss Bird both try to talk to the Baron at once and start shouting over each other. Then *he* starts to shout, spit flying through his moustache. He's loud enough for the boys to make out most of what he's saying. They hear:

Gretchen looks at the ground. Eventually, the Baron stops bellowing. He quietly says something to Miss Bird, who nods obediently and goes back into the garage. He follows her inside without looking at Gretchen, then slams the door behind him. Gretchen's mum stares at Gretchen and points at the house. Gretchen is crying. The boys look at each other.

"I think I've seen enough," says Ekam. "Let's go."

The boys are quiet on the way back to town. They freewheel down the hill, both lost in their thoughts. They stop their bikes at the canal bridge.

"What are you doing now?" asks Ekam.

"Dunno," shrugs Stick. "Mum's on a split shift and Dad's at work somewhere."

"Want to come to ours? Play GameBox?"

"Really?" says Stick. "Yeah! I'll have to tell Mum though."

"Just text her from my mom's phone."

Stick follows Ekam along the canal until they get to his block. They push their bikes into the lift.

Stick wrinkles his nose. "Standard lift smell," he says.

"Yep," says Ekam. "Like, who has time to wee in a lift?"

"A mini-wee? A *wee* wee?"

"Super-quick-wee!"

"Very good. Heroic. *Wee*-roic!"

The lift creaks open and they wheel their bikes along the balcony to Ekam's flat and lean them outside.

"Hello?" calls Ekam as he opens the door.

"Hey, doofus," says Jazz from inside. "Oh, hello, Stick!"

"Hey, Jazz."

"Where have you two idiots been?" she asks as Ekam raids the fridge. "All right, Ek, jeez! Leave some for the rest of us!"

They sit and eat, and tell Jazz their theory about Mr Jansari and then about what they saw at the mansion. Stick remembers overhearing Miss Bird on the phone when he hid behind the lockers, and tells them about how frightened she sounded.

"And when Birdy showed up in O'Leary's office with the laptop, he didn't seem too excited about her finding it," says Stick. "He just looked … thoughtful. And they were *not* very friendly to each other."

"Hmmm," says Jazz. "So Birdy is working with the Baron, and Jansari might be a *secret agent*?"

"Yeah," says Stick, "and 'the controllers' Gretchen was caught playing with must be for the HomeBots. It would

explain why ours was basically talking to me this morning
– it was her."

"And it definitely sounds like the Baron has something
big planned for the concert on Saturday afternoon," says
Ekam.

"But we have no idea *what* he's planning. *And* we
can't prove any of this. Urgh. My head hurts. Too much
thinking. What games do you have, Ekam?"

"I got the new Super Boy one out of the library," he
says. "Come on, I'll show you."

Super Boy VS The Kaos Kid

Four. Hours. Later.

The boys are still sitting in front of Ekam's mum's
massive TV, playing two-player Super Boy Adventures.
Stick is playing as the Kaos Kid, Ekam as Super Boy.
They're at a crucial point in the game, battling each other
on top of a collapsing volcano when the front door opens
and a happy voice calls out.

"Hello, hello! Where are my beautiful children?"

"Hi, Mom!" calls Ekam, without taking his eyes away
from the screen.

"Hello, poppet," she says, coming into the living room. "Oh, hello, who's this?"

Stick pauses the game and stands up to say hello. That's a lot of hellos.

"Hello, Mrs Kaur. I'm Stick." Stick smiles.

Ekam's mum looks at them.

"How long have you boys been sitting in front of that thing?"

"Not that long," says Ekam.

"Not long? Look at this boy's eyes, Ekam Singh! You're not fooling me. Switch it off this instant."

"But Mom!"

"Don't you 'But Mom!' me, young man. Off."

"Yes, Mom."

"That's better," she says. "Did you eat something, Stick?"

"Yes, Mrs Kaur, thank you."

"Aw, my good son," she says, ruffling Ekam's hair.

"*Only* son," says Jazz, appearing in the doorway. "Hope you're not too hungry, these two gannets ate most of what was in the fridge."

"That's all right, it's there to be eaten, Jasdeep love. Your mum know where you are, Stick?"

"Yes, Mrs— Oh, actually, no! I should go. Bye, Jazz! Bye, Ekam, see you Monday. Thanks for dinner, Mrs Kaur!" And off he goes.

Sunday soup

On Sunday, Stick wakes to the sound of rain. He wanders downstairs, yawning and scratching his bum. The house is quiet. Mum and Dad were still at work when he got back last night, and they've left again already. He puts the kettle on and goes into the living room. Bella is curled up on the couch, in her pyjamas. She's smiling as she messages someone on her phone and barely looks up to say good morning.

Stick takes his cereal upstairs and spends the morning copying pages from Super Boy Versus the Spider Princess. He thinks about the HomeBots as he draws, and about Gretchen and the Baron and Miss Bird. Are they really using the HomeBots to break everybody's stuff? It kind of seems like it. But why? He thinks and wonders and thinks some more, absent-mindedly drawing an extra two legs on the Spider Princess.

He imagines the Baron and Miss Bird in the control room, controlling HomeBots in people's flats and houses, pushing them into things. Knocking over TVs. Toppling radios into the sink. Unplugging freezers. Nudging bottles of wine out of windows. Pushing shoes into litter bins. Explains why they're always bashing into everything. Are they listening too? To everyone? He focuses on drawing again, getting lost in copying and colouring until Bella calls him down for lunch.

"I hear your momentary VidWire fame has been eclipsed by some random Year Eights singing the worst song ever written," says Bella.

"Mmm-hmm," says Stick, slurping on his soup. "I'm not *too* sad about it." He dunks some bread in his bowl.

"No," says Bella, smiling. "I expect not. Speaking of creepy robots, exactly why is there a bucket on ours?" she asks, watching the bucket slide across the kitchen floor.

"Dad's invention. A privacy setting,"

Bella nods. "Thought it might be his handiwork. Does he think it's watching him?"

"I'm not sure," says Stick, "but I think they're up to something." And he tells her about the weird conversation he had with it the day before, and the missing-not-missing-laptop, and what he and Ekam saw at the mansion, and about people's HomeBots breaking their stuff so they have to buy new things.

"What do you think?" he asks Bella.

"My brother, the conspiracy theorist," says Bella. "I think you need a hobby, doofus."

"Don't you think it's all a bit weird?"

"That my brother is whispering conspiracy theories in case the robot pushing a bucket around the kitchen hears him?" asks Bella. "No, not weird at all."

DETENTION DAZE

Stick wakes up late on Monday to Dad calling him from downstairs. He rushes through breakfast, then legs it out of the door and down the hill to school, running late again. Halfway there, jogging past the witchy trees, he remembers that he has detention – what will it matter if he's late? Plus he's already grounded.

He does arrive late, missing assembly and going straight to class. He daydreams his way through French and RE, trying to imagine what the Baron's Grand Evil Plan for the afternoon of the concert might be. What *exactly* is he up to? Using the HomeBots so people will buy more of his stuff? And how is Miss Bird involved? What would Super Boy, the world's greatest superhero detective, do? He needs more information.

```
More information?
```

"We need more information."

It's morning break. Stick closes his locker and turns round to see Nic, Milo and Ekam standing there. He looks at Nic. "More information about what?"

"About the HomeBots. The Baron. Everything!"

"I thought you didn't believe any of this?"

Nic fumes. "I didn't, until I found my GameBox outside in the rain yesterday, next to the HomeBot. HomeBots, it turns out, are waterproof. GameBoxes are not."

"Are you sure you didn't—"

"AARGH!" says Nic, "NO! Why would I put my GameBox outside? That stupid robot must've pushed it out when someone opened the door for the cat."

"So…"

"So now I believe you morons."

"Apology accepted," says Milo, grinning.

"Yeah, thanks, Nic. You're forgiven," says Ekam. He looks at Stick. "I told them what we saw at the Baron's mansion."

"OK," says Stick. "We know the Baron is planning something for Saturday night. So we have five days to figure everything out and stop him. We need a plan."

"Agreed," says Ekam. "Stick, can you keep a close eye on Birdy? Nic and me will head back to the mall and see if there's anything going on there, and Milo can observe Jansari to see if he's a secret agent."

"Ha!" says Milo.

"All right, bossyboots," says Nic. "Who put you in charge?"

"Do you have any better ideas?"

"No, yours seem sensible. But we could, like, take turns at being the leader?"

"Fine with me. You can be in charge tomorrow," says Ekam with a grin. "Milo? Stick? OK with you?"

They both nod.

The bell rings.

"OK," says Nic. "Listen, Stick. I've been in detention with Birdy before, here's what you need to do..."

At lunchtime, Stick makes his way to the ICT lab for detention. He arrives to find Sam there, not surprisingly. He takes a seat near the back, keeping his head down. Miss Bird skips in and smirks when she sees Stick.

"*Ah yes*, our new recruit. Make him feel at home, Sam. And do please try not to steal any of our stuff, will you, Stick? There's a good chap."

Stick looks up. He feels a pinprick in his chest, a small hot point of anger. *Gretchen's* the one who took the laptop. And Miss Bird *knows* this. Deep breath, Stick. He remembers Nic's advice: "Be nice".

"Yes, miss," he says with a forced smile. "I'm just going to get on with some homework. Thank you."

"Homework? Tsk. No, no, no. That's not how it works in here. Is it, Sam?"

"No, Miss Bird."

"Please explain to our *sticky*-fingered little friend here what we will be doing today. *Every* day, in fact."

And Sam does.

"She made you do what?" says Ekam. It's Tuesday morning and the boys are at Stick's locker again.

"No way," says Milo.

"It's true," says Stick.

"So let me get this straight," says Nic. "You spent all of lunchtime detention—"

"And afternoon," says Stick.

"—and afternoon, posting comments on VidWire? *Mean* comments?"

"Yep," says Stick.

"As yourself?" asks Ekam. "Like, 'Stick sez dis sux, frowny face, frowny face, thumbs down'?"

"No, not as myself! As made-up people. Fake people. At lunchtime I was Marjory, a grumpy jockey from Milton Keynes, and in the afternoon I was Winston, a disgruntled sign-painter from Newport. I'm not even sure what disgruntled means."

"Angry or dissatisfied," says Milo. "This is *crazy*. And … why?"

"No idea," says Stick. "I mean, some of the videos really were terrible, so it wasn't too difficult. One was about beards."

"Beards?" say the three boys at the same time.

"Yep. Some guy talking about putting oil in his. Or cream or something. And we had to post mean things in the comments."

"I never had to do that when I was in detention," says Nic. "What did you write?"

"That his beard looked like a toilet brush. Only I didn't write it, *Marjory* did."

"But ... why?" says Milo. "What's the point?" He frowns. "Wait. What does Birdy do while you're being nasty on VidWire?"

"She just sits there on her laptop, talking to herself. She was muttering something about packets. And a useless traffic sniffer?"

"Traffic *what*? Is that like some kind of insult?" says Nic. The boys all look at each other and shrug.

"Any luck with Jansari?" asks Ekam.

"Nope," says Milo. "In class he just teaches, and I can never find him at break. But if he's really a secret agent then he's probably not going to give himself away. Dead end, I reckon. Maybe there's a clue in the videos? What else did you write comments on?"

"Plenty," says Stick. "There was a beard video, a topknot video, one about craft tea, one about craft toffee, one about craft coffee, um … one about rolled-up jeans, one about bikes with no gears, one about latte art, one about tattoos, one about vegan burgers…"

Wednesday

By morning break on Wednesday, the boys have news. Ekam goes first. "So, we go to the mall yesterday—"

"Wait," says Nic, "I'm team leader today, let me tell it!"

"Cool, cool. Go for it, buddy." Ekam nods.

"So we go to the mall. And we see all these vans there—"

"Like the one we saw on Saturday, Stick."

"Eks! Let me tell it! So, they're all driving up in a line to unload at the back door, the one you unlocked, and guess what they're unloading?"

The boys look at him. Milo shrugs.

"Dunno. Ostriches? Herring? Portraits of the queen? It's a mall, mate, could be anything."

Nic rolls his eyes. "It wasn't *anything* though, was it? It was HomeBots. Hundreds of them. Thousands maybe."

"OK," says Stick, "but they do *sell HomeBots* at the mall."

"I know," says Ekam. "But there were *thousands*. Maybe ten thousand even, all stacked up behind the stage. He'd never sell that many."

"Unless," says Stick, thinking, "he's not planning to sell them at all... Milo, do you have a HomeBot?"

"Yeah, of course. We have two, one upstairs and one downstairs."

"Did you buy them?"

"Er ... I think they came free with something. The TV?"

"Ours came free with the GameBox," says Nic quietly. "My poor, dear, departed GameBox."

"Ours came with the sandwich toaster," says Ekam.

"And ours came with the TV. And Dad took the TV back, but they let him keep the HomeBot."

"So..." says Nic, "has anyone actually bought one? The Baron just gives them away?"

"And they're listening to everything we say..." says Milo.

"And they're breaking all our things, so we have to buy new stuff…" says Ekam.

"So the more people that have a HomeBot, the more money the Baron makes," says Stick.

"It's genius!" says Nic. The boys look at him. "I mean, evil genius, obviously."

"There is a certain … *elegance* to his scheme," says Milo.

"It's despicable," says Ekam. "I can't think of anything worse."

"I can," says Stick. "What if they don't just listen? What if they can *watch us* too?"

Miles away

Mum is in the kitchen when Stick gets home.

"All right, my little rascal? You keeping out of trouble?"

"Yes, Mum."

"How was detention today? Did you watch more stuff on VidWire?" Stick nods. "Honestly, you lot have it easy. In my day…" Mum carries on, and Stick zones out. He's thinking about the HomeBots. If they could get their hands on one, maybe they could dismantle it and see if it has a camera? But how would they get one?

"Are you listening to me, Stick?"

"Huh? Sorry, Mum, I was miles away."

His mum gets up from the table and comes over to give him a hug. "I was saying, poppet, why don't you invite those new friends of yours over one evening? You're still grounded, mind you. But it doesn't mean you can't have friends over."

Stick nods, excited. "Really, Mum?"

"Yes, really. What about tomorrow? I'm on a late but Bella will be here. She can make sure you don't destroy the place. Or open any locked doors, steal my laptop, that kind of thing."

"*Mum!* What about Dad?"

His mum chuckles. "Working I think, love. He's got some big project on."

"OK." Stick grins. "Thanks, Mum!"

The next day at the lockers, Milo is more excited than usual. "All right, Mystery Mates?"

"That is just *terrible*," says Nic, arriving with a big sports bag. "We are *not* the Mystery Mates."

"You're just jealous that you didn't think of it first," says Milo with a grin.

Stick laughs. "It is pretty bad, Milo."

Milo raises an eyebrow at him. "Not as bad as some of your comments on people's videos, is it, *Charlotte the Chocolatier* from *Chelmsford*? He puts on a squeaky voice. "'This little vintage clothes haul should truly be confined to the dustbin of history'."

"I don't sound like that! And I've had three days of trying to write mean things! I was trying out some pathos for a change."

"Pathos?" says Ekam.

"To elicit a feeling of pity or sadness," says Stick. "Belly was talking about it yesterday in English."

The boys nod. "Good one," says Milo. "Anyway, listen. I figured out why Birdy is getting you and Sam to put comments up on all those videos. It's because *she has her own!*"

"Her own comments?" says Nic.

"Nic! Seriously? Her own videos."

"What?"

"Yup. Miss Bird's Boss Beard Beautification. Miss Bird's Vintage Wardrobe Wonderland. Miss Bird's Vibrant Vegan Recipes. Miss Bird's Tip-Top Tattoo Tips. Miss Bird's Vinyl Voyage—"

"What?" says Ekam. "You're joking."

"Nope. She has videos on everything. Cheese. Funny-looking bikes. Rolled-up trousers. Black-and-white movies with subtitles. Something called normcore."

"How did you figure it out?" asks Stick.

"It was easy enough, Charlotte. I just looked at the comments under yours, and there was always a comment agreeing with you that had a link to one of Miss Bird's videos, always posted by the same people."

"Who?"

"Someone called A_Feathered_Friend, and Beak_Oz_Im_Worthit," says Milo.

"Oh dear," says Ekam. "That's Birdy, isn't it? Both of them. That's a bit sad."

"But why does she do it?" asks Stick.

Milo shrugs. "Clicks, probably. Everybody wants those clicks, baby!" He looks at Nic. "What's in the bag?"

Nic grins. "So we went back to the mall last night," he says, dropping his voice to a whisper, "and there were all these workers around the stage again. They were bringing in loads more HomeBots."

"What? More?!" says Stick.

"Yeah," says Ekam. "Big armfuls of them. Not even in boxes. There was one guy by the stage checking them, just saying 'Hey Homie' over and over again. Any that didn't respond went in the bin out the back."

"So?" says Milo.

"So…" says Ekam, nodding to Nic.

Nic unzips his sports bag. The boys look inside.

"Nice work," says Milo.

Inside is a shiny new HomeBot. It looks just like every other one, but shinier. Extra shiny.

"Incredible," says Stick. "And quite shiny."

"Let's take it apart! See if there's a camera inside!" says Milo.

"Yeah, but not here," says Ekam. "Where though?"

"Let's do it at mine," says Stick. "Tonight."

Detention. Again.

It's lunchtime detention. Again. Stick's already had a lesson with Miss Bird today and already had her picking on him with questions about things they haven't even covered yet. He drags himself back to the ICT lab and sits in front of his console. His reflection in the screen stares back at him.

Miss Bird arrives, clacking into the room on her heels. She dumps her handbag on her desk with a sigh, and hands a sheet of links to Sam and Stick. It's just the two of them today. Again.

LEARN BINARY! IT'S AS EASY AS 1, 10, 11!

Stick looks at the list of links and fake identities while he waits for his console to load. Why can't she just email this stuff to them? Typing the links in makes no sense to him, long strings of numbers and letters that he gets wrong half the time. He looks over at Sam, who's scratching her head. She's already tapped in the first address and is waiting for the clip to load. They haven't really spoken since the incident with the dogs a week ago. She's been quiet in detention. Just takes the lists and starts writing comments. Wait, is she putting up her hand?

Miss Bird gives Sam a cold stare over the top of her glasses. "Sam Devine, are you putting up your hand? In *my* detention? I hope you have a very good reason for doing so. One that's not going to land you in detention again next week." She glares. "Are you *quite sure* you want to do this?"

Sam looks back at the list of videos. Sam frowns. Sam thinks. Sam puts down her hand. Stick looks at the list. He looks over at Sam. He sees what's on her screen. It's Sam. On Sam's screen. What? He quickly types in the address for the first clip. It's for a video on *Sam's* vox pop channel, one of her Friday Factor interviews. He looks over at Sam again. She's just staring at the screen. He looks at Miss Bird. She's smirking like a pony after a big poo. She turns to look at Stick.

"Get to work," she spits.

He looks back at his screen.

What's he going to do?

What would *you* do?

He begins to type. He clicks and types and clicks, commenting on one video after the next after the next. By the time the bell rings for fifth period, his arms are sore from typing. On the way out, he runs to catch up with Sam.

"Sam," he calls. "Wait!"

Sam turns suddenly. "What do you want?" she snaps. "Just because we're in detention together, doesn't make us friends."

"Are you OK?"

She definitely does not look OK. She grabs Stick by the arm and drags him into an empty classroom, shutting the door.

"Listen, you—" she starts, shouting, but then stops and suddenly sits on the floor. She pulls her knees up to her chest and breathes in, a big deep breath. She sniffs.

"I'm listening," says Stick.

Sam sniffs again. "I worked really hard on those clips, you know? All those interviews and edits, and now the comments are all *nasty*."

"I know," says Stick.

"All that work. And I liked it too, asking people questions and stuff."

"Do you know why she makes us do it?"

Sam sniffs, and finally looks up. "No."

So Stick tells her.

And then they make a plan.

16 HACKING THE HACKERS

That evening, Stick is taking pizzas out of the oven when the doorbell rings. He shouts to his sister.

"Bella, can you get the door, please?"

He hears her thumping down the stairs and the click of the door.

Bella shouts back from the hallway. "Some little street urchins I don't recognize. Must be for you! He's in the kitchen, children."

Nic, Milo and Ekam file in.

"Delivery!" says Nic, dumping his sports bag on the kitchen table.

"Easy!" yells Jazz, appearing at the door. "They're not indestructible. Hi, Stick."

"Hi, Jazz," says Stick. "No babysitter?"

"Nope," says Ekam.

Stick puts the pizzas on the table and the gang starts to eat.

"What's in your bag, Milo?" asks Stick.

"One HomeBot, slightly dented," says Milo through a mouthful of four cheeses. "Stopped working. Our other one pushed it down the stairs. Looks like their appetite for destruction extends to each other." He swallows. "I thought maybe we could take this one apart too?"

The others nod. "Good idea," says Ekam.

"OK, let's do this," says Jazz. They clear away the plates and put the two HomeBots on the table next to each other. Jazz has brought a bag of her mum's tools, and the kids rummage through it to find some way of opening the robots. It proves tricky. There are no screws on the outside, and they look for seams where the pieces of the robot shell join together but there are none. Even the wheels are tucked inside.

"This is hopeless," says Nic. "The whole thing is glued together." He fishes in the tool bag, and pulls out a hammer. Before anyone can stop him, he starts bashing the old HomeBot with it.

"NIC! STOP!" shouts Milo. "That's not going to help! We need to find out what's inside, not smash them to bits! Jeez, you're such a traffic sniffer sometimes."

"You're a traffic sniffer!" Nic shouts back.

"Did you just call him a *traffic sniffer*?" asks Jazz.

"Yeah," says Nic, glaring at Milo. "He's a big traffic sniffer."

"You are!"

"No, you are!"

"Takes one to know one!"

Stick and Ekam look at each other. "All right, boys, calm down," says Ekam.

"Do you even know what a traffic sniffer is?" asks Jazz.

Nic sighs and puts down the hammer. "No. Not a clue. Stick heard Birdy say it in detention. Why, do you know?"

Jazz nods. "It's a way of seeing what people look at online. Like … like listening in on the conversation between someone's computer and the rest of the Internet."

"So you can find out what they're clicking on?" says Milo. "Like, properly spying? Cool."

"Why would she be talking about that?" Stick says. "Wait – Jansari's laptop! Could she have put a traffic sniffer on it to see what he's been looking at? How does it work?"

"Hang on," says Ekam. "When she had his laptop, she could have just looked at his history, right?"

Jazz shakes her head. "And everything else, but only if she knew his password ... but if she couldn't access the laptop then she *could* put a traffic sniffer on the school network to see what he's looking at online..."

"That's gotta be it. She needs proof that Jansari is a spy before they can do anything about it, and she's still looking," says Milo. "How do you know so much about this stuff, Jazz?"

"Just curious," says Jazz. "I'm a bit of a nerd." She grins proudly.

"Fair enough," says Milo.

"It's true," says Ekam. "Total nerd."

"What now?" asks Stick.

The Mystery Mates look around the table at each other.

Sorry, sorry, it's not a thing.

They hear the door opening and Stick's dad arrives.

"Evening, all! Full house! All right, lad?" he says, ruffling Stick's hair. "These your mates?"

Stick nods. The kids introduce themselves.

"Nic."

"Ekam."

—

"Milo."

"Jazz."

Stick's dad nods. "I'll do my best to remember all that." He looks at the HomeBots and the scattering of tools on the kitchen table. "What are you up to? Bit of homework?"

"We think the Baron is using the HomeBots to break people's stuff and we're going to open them up to see if we can find any proof," says Jazz.

"Ah yes, Stick mentioned your theory," says Dad, nodding. He scratches his chin. "You'll have to find out if they're receiving commands from somewhere then. You could do it with some kind of—"

"Traffic sniffer!" says Jazz.

"Er, yeah," says Stick's dad, impressed. "Exactly that. How did you…?"

"My sister is a nerd," offers Ekam.

Stick's dad nods. "Evidently. Hang on." He goes to the

hallway and rummages in the cupboard under the stairs, coming back with a tatty old bag full of cables and plugs and bits and bobs. He fishes around inside, pulls out an ancient-looking WiFi router and hands it to Jazz. "Here you go. If you can manage to get them open, you might be able to use this to intercept any info they're sending. Borrow Mum's laptop, Stick, but be careful with it." He yawns. "Long day, kiddos. I'm going to hit the hay. Don't stay too late. School in the morning, remember?"

"Yes, Mr Boy," say the kids in chorus.

"Night, Dad," Stick says, and turns to look at the HomeBots. "So how do we do this?"

"No, Nic, not the hammer."

"Isn't it obvious?" says Ekam. "Come on, Stick. I think watching all those VidWire clips has fried your brain."

Stick looks at him blankly.

Ekam wiggles his fingers and raises his eyebrows.

Stick facepalms. Then he gets to work on Milo's old HomeBot. It takes him about a minute to find a tiny hole in the case. He gets the end of his arm in, closes his eyes, sweats a bit and…

Click. He pops the case off the robot with a grin. The kids lean in. This is what they see:

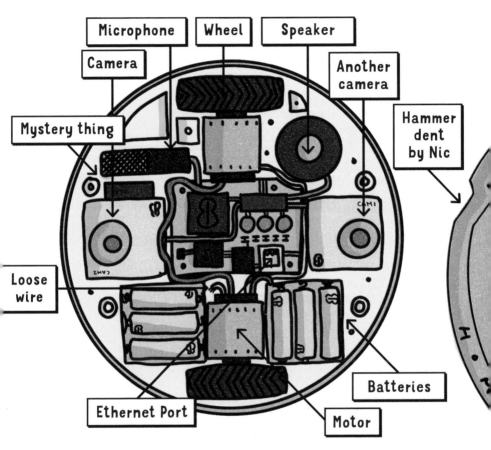

Microphone

Camera

Wheel

Speaker

Another camera

Mystery thing

Hammer dent by Nic

Loose wire

Batteries

Ethernet Port

Motor

"Knew it," says Stick.

"What the...? Cameras! Does this mean they're already watching us?" shouts Milo. "Stick, where's your HomeBot?" He looks around in a panic.

"It's OK, it's under that bucket in the loo," says Stick.

"Dad's privacy setting."

"OK. It has a camera. So now what?" says Ekam.

"Now," says Jazz, "we find out who's watching. Nic, hand me that red cable, please."

"And exactly who put you in charge?" says Nic.

"I'm taking my turn. Ekam told me about your system."

"Oh yeah. Fair enough. Here you go."

Jazz gets to work quickly, plugging in the router and connecting it to the HomeBot and the laptop. The boys watch. She downloads the software she needs and nods to Nic. "Cover the camera. And quiet, everyone, it's going to be listening." She connects the loose wire to the battery. The HomeBot beeps and boots up, its little lights flashing. Lines and lines of text appear rapidly on the laptop screen, strings of numbers and letters that don't make sense. Jazz nods, waits a few more seconds and pulls out the loose wire. The HomeBot shuts down.

"OK," says Jazz.

"What is it?" asks Nic.

"IP addresses," says Stick.

"Yep," says Jazz. She copies the first line of numbers and dots and pastes it into a browser window.

She hits return.

The page loads…

Oooh, the suspense!

It's a page about…

…

…moustaches.

"Huh?" says Jazz. "That makes no sense. Let me check the address again."

"Wait," says Milo . "I know that page! It's one of Birdy's. Look."

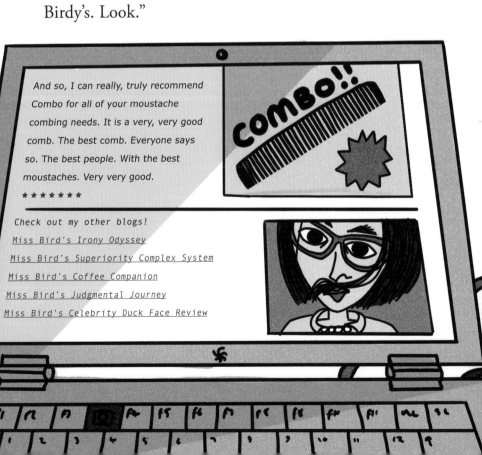

And so, I can really, truly recommend Combo for all of your moustache combing needs. It is a very, very good comb. The best comb. Everyone says so. The best people. With the best moustaches. Very very good.

★ ★ ★ ★ ★ ★

COMBO!!

Check out my other blogs!

Miss Bird's Irony Odyssey

Miss Bird's Superiority Complex System

Miss Bird's Coffee Companion

Miss Bird's Judgmental Journey

Miss Bird's Celebrity Duck Face Review

"Why would the HomeBot be looking at Birdy's videos?" asks Nic.

Ekam sighs. "It's not looking at her videos, Nic," he says. "It's sending her information. Can we see what it's sending?"

"No," says Jazz, clicking through the files. "I can't open these without a password."

Stick thinks. "Is it receiving information too?" he asks.

Jazz looks at the traffic log. "Yep," she says. "Two-way communication."

"Bingo. Explains how yours had that conversation with you on Saturday, Stick. Gretchen was using it to speak to you," says Ekam.

"Not just that. She's following me around. And watching too," says Stick, shuddering.

"I don't get it though," says Milo. "Jazz, you figured this out pretty quickly. Why hasn't anyone else? Why hasn't Jansari?"

"Maybe he can't open the files either. And maybe no one else is looking," says Jazz. "Everyone is too busy watching clips on VidWire. Nic?"

Nic looks up sheepishly from the laptop. He's opened

a new tab and is looking at a video of some kittens chasing a balloon with Jonny Vidwire's face on it.

Seriously, Nic.

"He won't get away with it for long," says Ekam. "Jansari will be able to crack the files sooner or later. Stick, can you open Milo's HomeBot?"

Stick quickly pops it open and they look inside.

"Looks exactly the same," says Nic.

"Wait a sec," says Jazz. "What's that thing?" She points at a little black box by one of the cameras.

"What is it?" says Milo.

"A satellite transmitter-receiver," says Jazz. "Says it on the side, there."

"They both have one," says Ekam, looking at the other HomeBot.

"Satellite? I thought they used WiFi?" says Stick. "Why does it… Of course – the satellite dish at the mansion, and the one on the mall! The Baron can use them to connect to the HomeBots… Could someone intercept that traffic?" He looks at Jazz.

"No way. Well, definitely not as easily as we just did," says Jazz.

"So why isn't the Baron controlling all the HomeBots like that already? The controllers at the mansion must work by satellite, right?" says Ekam.

Jazz nods. "Yes, but ... maybe not *all* of the HomeBots can be controlled by satellite yet. The Baron could be using the satellite dish at the mansion to test some of them first. When he's ready, the rest of the HomeBots will probably need some kid of upgrade to work by satellite though – new software and a reboot."

"Maybe our HomeBot has the new software?" asks Stick. "Dad said it wasn't working last Thursday – it wouldn't respond to him for hours."

"It might have been rebooting," says Jazz.

"For a few hours?" says Milo. "If people's HomeBots suddenly stop responding it would be bad for business. Not sure the Baron would risk that."

"It could be done while people are asleep," says Jazz.

"Someone's always awake," says Nic, yawning.

"Nic's right," says Ekam, "But what if people aren't paying attention to their HomeBots?" asks Ekam.

Stick nods. "What if they're distracted, you mean?"

"The concert," says Ekam. "Everyone that's not at the

mall will be glued to their TVs, watching Jonny Vidwire, and the Baron will have enough time to reboot the HomeBots."

"And he's going to give away thousands more of them at the concert. And he can control them all," says Stick. "Without anyone knowing. He can watch everyone. He can listen to our conversations. He'll know exactly what we want to buy without having to break anything." He thinks of his mum. "He's going to put all the other shops out of business."

"He can do much worse than that, Stick," says Milo. "What about looking at people's screens? Reading their emails? Seeing their passwords?"

"We need to tell someone what's going on," says Nic. "This is *actually* serious."

"Who's gonna believe us?" asks Milo. "Plus, the concert is the day after tomorrow. By the time we get anyone to believe that the Baron is an evil criminal mastermind who's breaking kitchen appliances and secretly spying on us, the concert will be over and everyone's HomeBots will be connected to the satellite system."

"Milo's right," says Stick. "We need to stop him. Ourselves."

Whoa. Where's the Stick from chapter one gone?

"Ha ha ha!" laughs Nic. "Oh, wait, you're serious?"

Stick nods. "Who's with me?"

Ekam nods, then Jazz, then Milo. Come on, Nic.

Nic nods.

"OK," says Stick. "Four kids against a mean teacher, a bully and her evil criminal billionaire father. We're going to need something else." He looks at the others. "We're going to need help."

TROUBLE IN TRAFFIC

"Bye, Mum!" calls Stick. It's Friday and he's running out of the door. He's arranged to meet the others before school starts and he's late, as usual. He hops on his bike and whizzes down the hill. He sees the satellite dish on top of the Mega Mall in the distance, hulking and grey in the morning drizzle. He zips past Jolly Goods and the other boarded-up shops, zooms over the canal bridge and whizzes down the little road with the witchy trees. He passes the high wall with the nasty spikes. He thinks about his keys on the other side. Was that really only last week?

When he gets to the school gates, the three boys are waiting. Nic has a face on. "You're late *again*," he says.

"It's OK," says Milo. "I'm in charge today, boys, and I'm cool with Stick being late. Don't mind him, Stick, he's just grumpy because his hair got wet."

"I'm *grumpy*," says Nic, "because Mum won't replace my GameBox. Says I should take better care of my stuff."

"Sorry," says Stick. "So what's the plan?"

"Well," says Milo. "If we're gonna prove anything about the HomeBots before the concert, we need to know what information they're sending to Birdy. And for that we need Birdy's password."

"Jazz tried to crack it after we got home last night, but she couldn't," says Ekam. "She's like a zombie today. You've got ICT first period, Stick, right? Do you think you can distract Birdy? Get access to her laptop?"

Stick nods. "Sounds impossible. I can try."

"Then what?" says Nic.

"Then the sooner we have the password, the sooner we get some proof and the sooner we can get the news out. We have to let people know what's going on *before* the concert," says Milo.

Traffic control

After assembly with an extremely over-excited Miss O'Leary, Stick heads to the ICT lab and takes his seat. He's seen quite enough of this classroom this week, he thinks. He turns his head to look out through the frosted glass. The world outside is a flat expanse of grey. Focus, Stick. You have a job to do here.

Miss Bird arrives and does the register. She doesn't look up when Stick calls "here". Weird. She usually has some kind of insult to offer whenever she sees him.

"OK, class, chapter forty-two of your textbooks."

The class flip through their books, right to the back, and Stick does the same. And then he sees it.

Chapter 42, Section 6: *Traffic Sniffing*.

Oh no.

OK, Stick. Don't panic.

Stick panics. He feels his heart thumping. *She knows, she knows, she knows*. How is he supposed to get the password now? And if she knows what they did, she's probably changed it already. But maybe it's a coincidence? It can't be. Can it?

"Now, class, *who* can tell me about *traffic sniffing*?" asks Miss Bird with an innocent smirk. "Hmmmm?" She taps her hard painted nails on the desk one at a time. She looks around the room.

Well, Stick. Here's something you know about in ICT, for once. Should he? He puts up his hand. OK. Miss Bird looks around the room. She looks at everyone but Stick.

"No one?" says Miss Bird. "Tsk."

"Miss—" he starts.

"Exercise forty-two point six, children. Please complete it by the end of the period. No questions. No speaking. Do not interrupt me unless something is on fire. Understood?" Everyone nods, including Stick. She still hasn't looked at him. This is bad. He looks at the exercise. It's pretty much what Jazz did with the HomeBot the night before. There's no coincidence. She knows.

A change of plans

"What?" says Nic. It's morning break.

"And then she just ignored you?" asks Ekam.

"Yep," says Stick, closing his locker.

"That's cold," says Milo. "How do we get the password now?"

"Forget it. She must've spotted the HomeBot when it uploaded files from your house, Stick. If she knows we're on to her she'll have changed her password. We need to go to the source," says Ekam. "We need to get to the controllers that connect to the satellite dish."

"What?" says Nic. "That's flipping impossible! You said there were savage dogs at the mansion! I am *not* going anywhere *near* savage dogs."

"Not at the mansion," says Stick, looking at Ekam. "You mean the massive one. At the mall."

"Yep," says Ekam. "And when we find the control room, you can open the door." Stick nods.

"Yeah," says Milo. "Sure. Once we get past security, actually find the control room in that ridiculous maze and then overpower whoever is inside. And then what? We smash all the controllers and then break the satellite dish with our bare hands and escape. No problemo."

"It does sound a bit ridiculous," says Nic. "To be fair."

Stick looks at the others. Ekam is chewing his lip. Milo is frowning and scratching his head. Nic is looking at himself using the selfie camera on his phone, fixing his hair.

Wait.

"What if…" says Stick. "What if we didn't have to smash anything?"

"What do you mean?" says Ekam.

"What if everyone *got rid of their own HomeBots*? That would stop the Baron's plan, right?"

"Yeah, no HomeBots means no spying, but why would people do that?" asks Milo. "They love their HomeBots. The song's not wrong."

"What if they didn't any more? They've already been spying on us all, right? So the Baron has recordings of everyone. What if we could get the recordings? We could put them on VidWire!"

"Forget VidWire," says Ekam.

"We could broadcast them. At the concert."

"Boom," says Stick. "Everyone will be watching."

"Whoa," says Milo. "I like this plan."

"Me too," says Nic. "As long as I get to pick any videos with me in them."

"We still need to get inside the Mega Mall though, without Birdy noticing. And the free concert tickets were all snapped up in about three seconds," says Ekam. "Did any of us get any?"

"Nope, but I bet Alannah has some," says Nic with a smirk. He elbows Ekam. "Why don't you ask her since you *love* her so much?"

Ekam blushes, but doesn't say anything. Milo and Stick chuckle.

"I can ask her," says Stick. "I'll see her in English."

"OK, good," says Milo. "The rest of us can go back to the mall tonight and see if we can find the control room."

18 CAUGHT

Stick is already in his seat in detention when Miss Bird arrives. She doesn't look at him or speak to him. This is horrible. Sam arrives and takes her seat. Miss Bird glares at her.

"Sam," she says. "Sam, Sam, Sam, Sam." Sam looks up.

"Have fun yesterday, did you? Commenting on your own videos?"

Sam looks down at the desk in front of her. "No, miss."

"*No, miss*," mimics Miss Bird, sneering like a satisfied hyena. "Lies," she spits.

Literally spits. On the floor of the ICT lab.

That. Is. Grim.

She stares at Sam, leaning in close. "You had some fun, didn't you, you and that other idiot?" she shrieks. By "other idiot", she probably means Stick, but she still hasn't looked at him. "Listen to this: 'Sam Devine's erudite questions on subjects ordinarily considered mere fluff, such as the Friday Factor, elicit responses from her interviewees that encourage a renewed appraisal of the contemporary consumption of pop culture. Five stars.

13/10 would recommend.' And this: 'Bonza clip, mate! Three thumbs up. Subscribe today. G'day!' It goes on. There are hundreds of these. Hundreds. All written during detention yesterday lunchtime and afternoon. All positive." She stares at Sam. "Did you think I wouldn't check? You were given clear instructions to write negative, spiteful comments on all clips. *All* clips. You ignored those instructions."

Sam doesn't say anything. She doesn't look up.

"Detention. Morning, lunchtime and afternoon. Two more weeks."

"But miss—"

Miss Bird holds up a hand. "Make that four weeks. And *shut up*. I've already contacted the VidWire admins to let them know that your account has been boosted by reviews written by fake accounts. I expect it will be suspended shortly. With any luck, it will be *deleted*." She grins. "Now back to work."

She hands them their lists. She looks at Stick, finally. She leans down to his level, looks him directly in the eye and hisses. Stick leans away from her as a shiver runs down his back.

Miss Bird leans closer and whispers, in a voice that's soft with threat. "I know you were behind this little *stunt*," she says. "And I know something else too. About you and your little friends. I have eyes *everywhere*. Think you've found something, do you? You haven't got a clue what you're *stuck* in, little boy."

She's interrupted by a knock on the door.

"Everything OK in here, Miss Bird?" It's Miss O'Leary.

Miss Bird stands up and turns to face Miss O'Leary, smiling. "Yes, Miss O'Leary, everything is simply *tickety-boo*." She claps her hands. "I was just saying to Sam and Stick how I am *so* looking forward to the concert tomorrow night. Aren't we all? Won't it be *fun*? Our school, chosen to represent Little Town on such a great occasion! How marvellous. Whatever shall I wear?"

"Yes!" says Miss O'Leary. "You know, I was wondering the same thing myself. Have you been to Sew Special? I hear they have some wonderful new styles…" She takes Miss Bird by the arm and leads her out of the room. "Won't be a moment, children – just borrowing Miss Bird for a spot of fashion advice."

Stick looks over at Sam. "Sam, I—"

"You what?" snaps Sam. "You've made it worse! I should never have listened to you!"

"I thought—"

"You thought what? You didn't think! You thought you'd show how brave you are, have some fun? Look what you've done."

Stick doesn't say anything. His throat feels tight.

"It doesn't matter to you, does it? If things get too much then Mummy and Daddy will just take you out of school. Mummy and Daddy will make everything better. Not everyone has it that easy. Making videos is the only thing I actually look forward to, and now it's gone."

"What about bullying?" ventures Stick. "You love being a bully."

"Not any more! People change, Stick! I only did it because I wanted a friend. Gretchen was the only one who would talk to me when I started school here. Do you know what it's like to be different?"

Stick looks at her.

"Sorry, of course you do," says Sam.

"No, I'm sorry," says Stick. "You're right. I didn't think

about what would happen if we got caught. I … I wanted to help."

"Well, you didn't." Sam sniffs. "Thanks for nothing. This is *hopeless.*"

"We could just report her," says Stick. "She's basically doing the same thing."

"Tried it already," says Sam. "No dice."

Stick frowns.

"Sorry," says Sam. "It didn't work. *Insufficient evidence.* Besides, who'd believe a kid in detention over a teacher? She'd just deny everything."

"What if…" says Stick. "What if she wasn't just a teacher?"

"Huh?" grunts Sam. "That doesn't make any sense." They hear the quick clatter of Miss Bird's heels in the corridor.

"I'll explain afterwards," whispers Stick.

The Missing Bottom

Stick has been enjoying English classes way more than he expected, and today Mr Bell does not disappoint. They're on Act IV, scene ii, and the players are discussing the missing Bottom and the appearance of a strange ass-headed monster in the woods. It's hilarious, obviously, but Stick likes that the characters all have nice things to say about Bottom and are sad to be missing their friend.

When the bell rings, he says goodbye to Alannah before he realizes that he's forgotten to ask her about the concert tickets. He runs out after her. "Hey, Alannah!"

He catches up with her, just as Ekam appears.

"Did you ask her?" says Ekam.

Stick shakes his head.

"Ask me what?" says Alannah, tucking a strand of hair behind her ear. She looks at Ekam.

Ekam blushes. Stick looks at both of them.

"You ask her," he says.

"Yes?" says Alannah.

"Do you have any tickets for the concert?" asks Ekam.

"What? I ... um, that wasn't what I ... maybe, yeah. Why? I thought you only liked football?"

"I like other things," says Ekam, looking defensive.

"What, like songs about HomeBots?" asks Alannah, raising one eyebrow.

"What? NO! That song was the WORST!" says Ekam.

"I know, right?" says Alannah, looking relieved.

Stick chuckles.

"What's going on then?" says Alannah. "Is this something to do with your Mystery Mates thing?"

Ekam frowns. "That's not a thing."

"I don't know," says Alannah, laughing. "I heard Nic saying it the other day. Sounded kinda like a thing to me."

Stick and Ekam both shake their heads and sigh.

"Come on," says Alannah. "Spill. I'll help you out if you tell me *everything*."

Stick looks at himself in the mirror.

"This is never going to work," he says.

"I don't know," says Nic, shoving Stick out of the way to admire himself. "I think we look *pretty cool*. Like a *cool band*."

"We do not look like a cool band," say Ekam and Milo together.

"Yeah, we do," says Nic, "The Mystery—"

"No!" says everyone else in the not-cool not-band. Everyone includes Stick, who is wearing an all-white suit with shoulder pads, purloined from Alannah's mum's wardrobe, topped off with a blond wig borrowed from her dad's collection. Next up is Nic, in a white T-shirt, jeans and leather jacket combination, followed by Ekam, in a suit he found at home and that sort-of fits him. Milo is wearing denim dungarees accessorized with flip-flops and a serious scowl.

"Remind me why I agreed to do this?" says Milo, as Alannah puts a clip in his hair.

They're in Alannah's flat, on the afternoon of the

concert. Alannah is trying to make them look co-ordinated. So far she's tried waistcoats, headbands, bracelets and baseball caps. She's hoping matching hairclips will do the trick.

"Because, Milo," she replies, "we don't have concert tickets, and there are seven of us. Four boys in the band, a manager, a choreographer, and a stylist, moi. We're going to get backstage, locate the controllers, find whatever the HomeBots have been recording and broadcast it, ruining the Baron's plans. And because purple is *so* your colour." She winks at him. "Ekam, you're next."

you're lucky enough to be different— don't ever change . T.S.

Stick looks around. Jazz and Sam are at the desk, hunched together over Alannah's laptop. He's glad he asked Sam for help. She wasn't convinced at first but the others agreed without hesitation.

"How are we doing on the blueprints for the mall?" he asks.

"Not very well," says Jazz. "Can't find anything. It's like he just made up the building as he went along."

"That would explain the avant-garde architecture," says Milo.

"Avant-garde?" says Stick.

"Unorthodox. Experimental. Unfamiliar," says Sam. "But I think Milo is being ironic. He's saying the architecture is avant-garde, which could be a compliment, but he means it in an insulting way. Meant to be funny."

Everyone looks at Sam, and then at Milo. Milo nods. "Exact-a-mundo. Sam gets it."

Stick smiles. "OK. But even in an avant-garde Mega Mall, the room with the controllers has to be somewhere near the satellite dish, right?"

"Yeah. Could be. Or in the basement. Anywhere really," says Jazz.

"Hmmm," says Stick, remembering the satellite dish on

the Baron's garage. "But the satellite dish has to connect to the control room… If we follow the cables from the dish, will we find it?"

Sam and Jazz look at each other. "In theory, yes," says Sam.

"Well, that's the best we've got. I say we start at the satellite dish," says Stick.

"You're in charge, buddy," says Ekam. "I'm with you."

"Agreed," say the others, together.

Stick nods. "Let's hope our disguises work."

Back to square one

The disguises don't work. No chance. The security guard at the entrance to the backstage area is reluctant to believe that they're Jonny Vidwire's secret support act, and when they start arguing amongst themselves about their band name the whole thing quickly falls apart. The security guard folds her arms and then growls at them until they leave. So now they're sitting on a kerb in the town square. Back to *square* one.

This is a disaster. They have to stop the Baron's plan or Stick's mum could lose her job. And the other people who work in shops. And he'll start properly spying on people. Maybe they should've talked to Jansari?

"Isn't there another way in?" asks Alannah.

"Nope," says Ekam. "We've been all around the building. The only other doors without security are up there."

High above the massive screen there's a balcony and above that is the massive satellite dish. It's *miles* away. Stick wishes he could stretch and stretch until he was tall enough to just reach over and pluck the satellite dish off the top of the mall. He squeezes his eyes really tight and concentrates hard… He wobbles slightly.

Wait.

That was something.

He holds his breath and concentrates again.

Wait for it…

POP.

His head is a triangle.

"Cool," says Alannah.

Stick sighs.

"Thanks."

"Oi oi!" says a voice.

"Why so glum, chum?"

Stick looks up. He gets to his feet and dusts off his trousers. "Hey, Eric."

"You lot going to the concert? That why you're all dressed up? Nearly didn't recognize you as a triangle. Oh, 'ello, Sam, didn't see ya there!"

"Hi, Mr Fernandez," says Sam.

"We don't have tickets," says Stick.

"Oh-dear-oh-dear-oh-dear," says Eric. "But that's all right. I can sort you out. How many are you? One, two, free, seven." He puts his hand in the inside pocket of his jacket, pulls out a stack of glossy black cards and counts them out. There you go – VIP passes." He points up. "Gets you on the balcony an' all."

Stick is speechless.

Alannah steps in. "Thank you, Mr Fernandez."

"Don't mention it. Perk of the job."

"You work for the Baron?" asks Stick, finding his voice.

"That geezer? Never. Don't trust him. I work for Mr Vidwire. Head of security. Speaking of which, I'm late. I best go make sure the little fella's secure. Enjoy the show!"

"Let's keep our disguises on," says Stick, as they go through the VIP queue and into the mall. "Birdy is gonna be looking for us."

Inside the mall, everybody is moving in the same direction. All the shops are open now: Baron Ben's Batteries, Baron Ben's Brassieres, Baron Ben's Bunting… It looks like the Baron has a shop for everything. Buy One Budgie, Get a HomeBot Free! Two HomeBots Free With Every Freshly Plucked Banjo! And so on. And everyone is shopping. There are HomeBots in the window of *every shop*. Watching *everyone*.

"Great," says Milo. "If Birdy is watching, she's going to find us in no time. We need to move fast."

"This way," says Sam, leading them to the escalators. Another burly security guard tries to stop them but they're quickly ushered through when he sees the VIP passes. "Look," says Sam, pointing from the escalator.

The others look down and see the stage below them. The massive screen behind it is still showing the same ad for the HomeBot with Jonny Vidwire's grinning face and sparkly teeth. Every seat at the front is already taken, rows of eager faces staring at the empty stage, slurping on their Sippy Shakez.

"This way!" says Nic, heading towards another escalator, this one painted gold.

"Tasteful," says Alannah.

The escalator brings them up on to the balcony. Bingo. They slip into the crowd of VIPs.

"OK," whispers Stick. "We need to find a way up to the satellite dish, and then into the control room. Try not to attract attention or look suspicious. Nic?"

He frowns at Nic, who's managed to grab eight canapés and already has four in his mouth.

"Dude," says Milo.

Nic shrugs. "Imhfs fhungry."

They look around, splitting up and dodging between tuxedoed and high-heeled guests, circling through the crowd and meeting again at the entrance.

"Anything?" asks Stick. The others shake their heads. "Flip." He looks up at the satellite dish. It's not even that far away… He touches the wall, but it's too smooth to climb. He looks around.

The party guests are having a great time, throwing their heads back and laughing at each other's jokes. Stick walks to the edge of the balcony and looks out down at the town square, at the little pond with the ducks and the tiny playground far, far below. He remembers his dad pushing him on their swing at their old house. Swinging back and forth, higher and faster...

"Milo!" says Stick. "Tangential velocity!"

Milo looks at him. "What?"

"Tangential velocity. You swing me round and up to the dish!"

"NO WAY, dude. That's ridiculous! What if I miss?"

"You won't. And even if you do, I'll be fine. I'll just fall to pieces and put myself back together again."

"You can do that?" says Alannah.

Stick nods. "Sam knows," he says.

"'S true," says Sam. "I've seen it."

"Whoa," says Nic.

"I don't know..." says Ekam. "It's a long way down from here. Are you sure about this?"

"Sure I'm sure. I'll be fine. Probably."

"Won't everyone notice?" says Jazz.

"Not if there's a distraction," says Sam. "Ready to sing, boys?" She grabs Ekam and Nic and starts moving through the crowd to the other side of the balcony.

"Distinguished guests!" she says at the top of her voice. "Have we got a *special treat* for you! To whet your appetites for tonight's concert, we bring you a special a capella performance by Little Town's latest pop sensation, pop-up popstars, if you will…" The crowd chuckles, and everyone turns towards Nic and Ekam.

"Quick," says Stick, slipping out of his suit and standing straight with his arms by his sides. "Let's do this. I'm ready."

"Wait…" says Milo.

"Please put your hands together for the HomeBot Boyz!"

The crowd cheers and claps, everyone eager to see the show.

"Now," says Milo. He grabs Stick by the ankles and holds him out over the balcony. Before Stick has time to change his mind, Milo begins to swing him round and round, faster and faster and faster and then … he lets go.

Stick goes sailing up

and up …

and time slows down…

He opens his eyes.

HE'S FLYING!

He sees the satellite dish, straight ahead. Excellent work, Milo. He hears a wailing noise below him, straight-up *awful*. Excellent distraction, boys.

He flies up past the rim of the satellite dish and reaches for the sticking-out antenna bit. He grabs it and swings round once, landing softly in the dish. He quickly runs to the edge and hops off. He spots some thick red cables connected to it and follows them to a small gap in the wall. There's just enough space for him to slip through and into a narrow space filled with even more cables and wires. He climbs down and follows the red cables along a tube like an air-conditioning vent, just wide enough to fit his head.

Best not get stuck, Stick. He holds his breath and inches along. There's daylight up ahead, and he can feel a breeze on his face, but then the cables drop through a hole in the bottom of the vent. Is this it? He lies down and looks through the hole and into the room below, filled with screens and computer equipment. The controllers! *Bingo.*

The room below Stick is massive. One whole wall is nothing but screens, rows and rows and rows of them, stacked high from the floor to the ceiling. Every screen is showing – you guessed it – a live stream from a HomeBot somewhere in Little Town. Most of them are pretty boring, but there's one of Mr Bell watching a Jonny Vidwire music video, singing along, using a hairbrush as a microphone. He actually looks pretty good.

A voice buzzes in over the intercom. *"ALL STAFF, REPORT BACKSTAGE. POSITIONS FOR INTRO. ALL STAFF."*

Focus, Stick. All you need to do is get down from the ceiling, get some of those clips and then upload them to VidWire before the show starts. Without anyone seeing you. No problem.

What would Super Boy do? First things first: get out of the ceiling and into the control room, preferably without being seen.

Stick pokes his legs through the hole
in the floor, ready to lower himself into the
room below. The only sound he can hear
is the soft hum of computers. He can't see
the whole room, but he's going to have to
risk it. He slips his body through the hole
and swings by his arms from the edge. He's
hanging in front of the wall of screens, a
long way from the floor. What now?

He turns his head to look behind him.
He sees stacks and stacks of computers
that reach almost to the ceiling and a huge
console with loads of wires and screens,
like something from NASA. But a tacky
version, made by Baron Ben. There are lots
of little screens surrounded by buttons,
and what look like GameBox controllers
in front of each one. There are crusty old
milkshake cups and half-eaten burgers
everywhere. And there, sitting in the
middle of it all with her arms folded and a
grin on her face like a farting warthog, is
Miss Bird.

Aaah …

"I've been expecting you, Mr Boy," says Miss Bird with a sneer. She sucks her teeth, and then scrapes something from between them with a pointy fingernail.

Is that a bit of old chip? Ugh.

Stick wobbles. What now? He's losing his grip, and it's a long way down. He tries to pull himself back up into the ceiling but his arms are too tired and he slips and falls … and falls …

... and hits the floor with a clatter.

Ow. Why don't they put carpets in these evil control centres?

In a flash, Miss Bird is out of her chair and clacking across the floor.

Get up, Stick!

He looks around frantically for his arms, but he can't see them. In a second, Miss Bird's face is above his, leaning in so close that he can see the hairs in her nostrils.

"*Stuck*, Stick?" she sneers, cackling at her own bad joke. "Do allow me to be of assistance!"

A little tied up

Two minutes later Stick really is stuck. He's sitting, tied to a chair. His arms and legs hurt. So would yours if Miss Bird had tied them in knots behind your back. He's trying really, really, really hard not to cry. He wants to shout at Miss Bird, shout at her to let him go, shout at her to stop, shout at her that this is not fair and she's not allowed to do this to a child but he can't because she's taped over his mouth and he can't say a word. Miss Bird can though, and it seems like she won't ever shut up.

Stick doesn't look at her. He needs to figure out a way to escape. He wriggles his arms and legs but the knots are tight and messy and everything really hurts. Deep breath, Stick. Try not to panic. Miss Bird is still yapping.

"It doesn't matter what you know because in a few hours it will be impossible to prove anything. Your little trick with the traffic sniffer was clever, I'll admit, but as soon as everyone's HomeBot gets its upgrade we can watch whoever and whatever whenever we like and *no one will ever know*. No more pushing toasters into the sink. Oh no. We can look at the really juicy stuff. Emails. Passwords. Credit cards. *Bank accounts*." She rubs her hands together with glee.

"Why should we get people's money by making them buy stuff when we can just take it from them directly? A little bit from everyone, not so much that anyone will notice, but enough to make me rich. A HomeBot in every home, and all of them controlled by me!"

They were right. But why is she telling him all this?

"Why am I telling you all this? Because … I can! Because no one will ever believe you! They won't believe that idiot Jansari either. He thinks he's so flipping smart…"

Stick struggles. She's wrong. Someone will believe him. Mum and Dad will.

"What are you thinking? That Mummy will believe her *little twiglet*? Ha! Doesn't matter, does it? Without any proof, she'll be laughed at. Forget it," says Miss Bird with a sneer. "You just sit *tight* until all this is over."

She steps behind his chair, pulls at the knots in his arms and then turns the chair to face the wall of screens. Every seat in the arena is now full, and the audience are happily sitting and chomping on their chips as they stare at the still-empty stage.

"Not long to go now," says Miss Bird. She looks in a hand mirror and reapplies her bright red lipstick. "How do I look?" There's a knock at the door. "Right on time," says Miss Bird, grabbing her handbag and marching towards the exit. She opens it and Stick looks over.

It's Gretchen, wearing a horrible mauve dress.

"Dad says you need to come—" she starts, but stops when she sees Stick. "What's going on? What's he—"

"Nothing!" snaps Miss Bird. "Go!" She pushes Gretchen out and slams the door behind them.

The dark, heavy feeling is back with a vengeance, swirling inside Stick until it fills him up completely. He sobs and gulps, the tears coming fast and hot. They can't stop the Baron now. He'll get richer and richer and never get caught. Things can't get any worse.

Wait, that reminds him of something. What is it? Was it something Mum said? Yes!

When things can't get any worse, they can only get better.

He laughs through his snots and his tears. It sounds silly. But he lifts his head. He looks around. There must be something he can do. First things first: get out of this chair.

21 WHAT?

Five minutes later, he's still in the chair.

No matter how hard he tries, he can't undo the knots. He's tried concentrating. He's tried relaxing. He's tried wriggling. He's tried jumping. This is hopeless. He hears a noise at the door and looks over. Is Miss Bird coming back? That is not what he needs.

The door opens, but it's not Miss Bird. It's Gretchen. She closes the door behind her and walks over to Stick. What's she going to do?

She looks at him. She's not wearing her usual grin. Stick looks back at her and tries to shuffle his chair away.

"Stop," says Gretchen.

Stick stops.

"Take a deep breath," says Gretchen.

Stick shakes his head.

Gretchen sighs. "Just do it." She pauses, then adds, "*Please.*"

What is going on?

He takes a deep breath.

In a swift movement Gretchen puts one hand on his shoulder and rips the tape off his mouth with the other.

"Oh shush, it'll stop hurting in no time," says Gretchen, crouching behind Stick and untying his arms and legs.

"Ow!" says Stick. "That hurts too!"

"My sincere apologies," says Gretchen. "These knots are simply *dreadful*. But I am, as you know, the bully. Hurting is very much my line of business. Now get up."

Stick gets up and immediately falls over. Great. He swaps one arm and one leg and gets to his feet, rubbing his sore arms. He looks at Gretchen. She's busy at the main control console.

"Why did you untie me?" he asks.

"Because, Stick –" she looks him dead in the eye – "I think it's about time I stood up for myself too. Don't you?"

Stick nods, surprised.

"We don't have much time," says Gretchen, quickly typing something on the controller. "As soon as my sister notices I'm missing she'll know something is up. Where are the others?"

Stick looks at her, confused. "You're helping us?"

"Yes, unless you're tied up in a chair in the HomeBot control room just for fun and not with the intention of putting an end to my dad's evil plans? Now, where are the rest of them? Look –" She points to the wall of screens, all of them now showing feeds from HomeBots inside the mall.

"They should still be on the balcony," says Stick, scanning the video streams. "There!" He points to a view of the crowd on the balcony, where several of the well-dressed guests have their fingers in their ears. A small child is weeping.

"Wow. OK," says Gretchen. "I'll lead them here." She taps in a command on the keyboard and picks up one of the GameBox controllers. Sam appears on the main screen, and Gretchen drives the HomeBot at her, crashing into her foot. Sam looks down. Gretchen flips a switch on the console and they hear what the HomeBot hears, which is some really, truly bad singing and Sam saying, "What the…?" as she raises her boot above the HomeBot…

"STOP!" shrieks Gretchen, grabbing a nearby microphone. "WAIT!"

Sam stops. She leans down and stares at the HomeBot. "Sam, it's me, Gretchen. I'm with Stick, in the control room. I can lead you here if you follow the HomeBot, but you have to come now!"

Sam shakes her head. "I don't trust you."

Stick grabs the microphone. "Sam, it's me! It's Stick!"

"You realize that the voice is the same, right?" says Sam. "How do I know that's not Gretchen saying that? Or anyone else? You could be Birdy. Or even the Baron."

"Sam! It's me! I can prove it! I know that you love vox pops and you know what irony means and you're afraid of Winnie and—"

"Who's Winnie?" asks Gretchen.

"Never mind!" say Sam and Stick together.

Sam looks hard at the HomeBot, then stands up and sticks her fingers in her mouth, letting out a loud and fierce "**FWWWWWWWWWWWWWPPPPP PPPPPPPPPPPPPPPPPPPPPPPPP!**" followed by a bellow of "SHOW'S OVER, FOLKS! We need to get our performers backstage ASAP! Thank you all for your attention, enjoy the rest of the afternoon! This way, please, HomeBot Boyz, follow me! *Now!*"

"Go-go-go!" says Stick.

The HomeBot leads the gang off the balcony and back to the escalator, going as fast as Gretchen can make it. Over the microphone, Stick can hear Sam explaining things to the others as they rush to keep up. Gretchen sends the HomeBot bouncing down the escalator steps and through the crowded corridors, shouting at the confused audience to jump out of the way.

In less than two minutes she stops, crashing the HomeBot into a door.

Thump.

Stick looks at the door of the control room.

"They're here?"

"Yep," says Gretchen. "And I have to go." She looks at him. "Thank you, Stick." She runs to the door, opening it and legging it out past the others.

"What—" says Stick, but she's gone before he can finish his question.

"How the…?" asks Ekam.

"Dude!" says Milo. "*What* is going on?"

"Stick," says Nic, "do you want the rest of that burger?"

Seriously, Nic.

"Wow," says Alannah, looking at the wall of screens. "What do we do now?"

Jazz and Sam are already sitting at a controller each, tapping and clicking. "We find a way to broadcast the video recordings from the HomeBots, and then we get out of here," says Sam.

"How do we do that?" asks Milo.

Sam and Jazz look at each other. "We'll find a way," says Jazz.

"What about the rest of us?" asks Alannah. "What do we do?"

Everyone looks at Stick. "You're in charge, buddy."

Stick looks around. On screen, the audience are screaming and jumping to their feet as Baron Ben's face appears on the big screen.

Time is running out. Think, Stick!

Thump.

Thump.

Thump.

Everyone turns to look at the door.

"SECURITY! OPEN UP!"

"I think," says Stick, "we need an escape plan."

"How long is it going to take to get the broadcast running?" asks Stick.

"A couple of minutes," says Sam.

Thump.

Thump.

Thump.

THUMP.

THUMP.

"OK, we can do this," says Stick. "The door is locked from the inside, so they can't get in, but it means we can't get out either. Everyone jump on a controller and take charge of a HomeBot. Let's see who's outside."

In a couple of seconds, Alannah has a HomeBot under control, the same one Gretchen crashed into the door. She brings its video feed up on the wall of screens in the control room.

"Uh-oh," she says.

"Miss Bird must've followed Gretchen!" says Stick. "We need to get them away from the door – everyone, get more HomeBots here!"

The gang works quickly, selecting HomeBots on their screens and racing them to the control room. Within a few minutes they have the security guards surrounded.

"OK," says Stick. "Let's do this!"

As soon as they begin, the adults stop kicking the door and start kicking the HomeBots instead.

"It's not working!" says Alannah. "We need more HomeBots!"

"We need another way out," says Ekam, concentrating on his screen. "We won't be able to distract them for long."

"How did you get in?" asks Milo, frantically bashing the buttons on his controller.

"Through there," says Stick, pointing up at the hole in the ceiling. "It's too high though."

Milo looks around and spots the stacks of computers. "We could reach it from up there! Can we move them?"

"We can try!" says Stick. "Nic, keep attacking with the HomeBots. How are we doing with the video feed, Sam?"

"Nearly there! Oh…"

A huge cheer suddenly erupts from the arena, so loud they can hear it through the walls of the control room. Even the security guards stop kicking the door and look around. Sam flicks through the video feeds from the HomeBots and brings the stage up on the wall of screens.

"Come on," says Stick, and the boys run to the stack of computers nearest the hole and start to push.

"It's too heavy!" says Milo. "Sam, we need you!"

Sam looks at Jazz.

Jazz nods. "I've got this. Go."

On stage, Jonny Vidwire is about to introduce the real HomeBot Boyz as Miss O'Leary ushers them onstage, beaming happily.

"LET'S GET STRAIGHT TO THE SONG YOU'VE ALL BEEN WAITING FOR, SHALL WE?" shouts Jonny, over the screams of the audience.

The crowd roars even louder, almost drowning out the thumping at the door.

"IT'S THE SONG YOU KNOW AND LOVE, THE OVERNIGHT VIDWIRE SENSATION, FROM LITTLE TOWN HIGH SINGING 'I LOVE MY HOMEBOT, IIIIT'S THE HOMEBOT BOYZ!'"

"Oh, I love this song!" says Nic, still busy smashing HomeBots into the security guards' ankles.

Homie homie HooooooomeBot,
I love myyyy HomeBot...

In the control room, there's a horrible crunching sound as the door finally begins to fall apart. The kids push as hard as they can, but even with Alannah and Nic helping, the stack doesn't budge. One of the security guards has got his foot stuck in the broken door, slowing them down. "Jazz, we need your help! NOW!" shouts Ekam.

"Got it," says Jazz. She looks up at the screen and taps the space bar on her keyboard. As she runs to help the others, the screen above the stage changes from a close-up of the band to a split screen of hundreds of video recordings from the HomeBots, flashing through clip after clip.

The HomeBot Boyz try to keep singing, but it's impossible over the wails of the audience.

In the control room, Stick looks at the others. "All together – PUSH!" They push, and the stack of computers wobbles and then slides across the floor, stopping under the hole in the ceiling. "Go!" shouts Stick, and they quickly clamber up and into the vent. "Head towards the light!"

Behind them, they hear a massive crunch and the cheers of the security guards as the door gives way. They hear Miss Bird in the control room, screaming like a vulture with indigestion.

Onstage, Jonny Vidwire shouts into his microphone, "HEY, HEY, HEY! DISTINGUISHED GUESTS, IT APPEARS THAT THERE HAS BEEN SOME KIND OF TECHNICAL MALFUNCTION, I'M SURE EVERYTHING WILL BE A-DIDDLY-OK IN A FEW MOMENTS!" The sound of his very worried voice fades as the gang crawls quickly along the air-conditioning vent.

"This way," says Stick, slipping past the others. "We should be outside soon... Oh. *Awesome*."

"What is it?" says Sam.

Stick looks over his shoulder and grins. "It's the slide! Come on!" He wriggles out of the end of the vent and on to the slide. He whizzes down first, spinning round and round the building, down and down until he pops out at street level. People are already rushing out of the mall in disgust, giving interviews to the press and TV crews outside. Sam, Alannah, Nic, Milo, Ekam and Jazz tumble out of the slide and join Stick.

"Now what?" asks Ekam, looking at Stick.

"Now we slip quietly away, I guess—"

"HEY! STOP THOSE KIDS!" shouts the smallest of the five security guards, struggling to free himself from the end of the slide.

"RUN!" shouts Stick.

They run through the crowd and across the square, leaping over shrubs and flower beds.

"Oh no," says Sam. "Is that the Baron's car?" She points at the limousine that's speeding around the square, on its way to intercept them. Behind them, the security guards are hurling shoppers out of their way as they get closer and closer. In front of them, the limo screeches to a halt as they reach the edge of the square, blocking their way.

Before they can run, the window of the car rolls down. Behind it is a face Stick recognizes.

"Get in, doofus."

`Your driver has arrived`

"What the…?" says Stick, slamming the door of the limo shut as they zoom away from the square, tyres screeching. "What's going on?"

"We're in a limo," says Nic, already handing out snacks from the mini bar. "Popcorn, Sam?"

A screen behind the driver whirrs down, and Bella turns around. "Calm down, little bro. This is my friend Maeve," she says, nodding towards the driver, who catches his eye in the rear-view mirror and nods. "All right, kid?"

"Yeah," says Stick, looking around. Everyone looks a bit dazed and out of breath, except for Nic, who's happily munching on a packet of crisps and trying to get the TV to work. "Why are we… How did you…?"

"Maeve's just got a job driving Baron Berk's limo at weekends," explains Bella. "It's her first day."

"Might be her last," says Maeve, looking in the side mirror at the security guards galloping behind her. She pulls hard at the wheel, sending the back of the car swinging in a wild arc until it bounces off the kerb and back into the road.

"Awesome," says Milo from the floor.

"Sweet," says Ekam, untangling himself from the others and hopping into a seat beside Stick. "Belt up, bozos."

Bella continues. "We saw the commotion outside the mall and I figured it might have something to do with you conspiracy theorists, so I wasn't too surprised to see you legging it across the square, and Maeve was happy to pick you up."

Maeve grins into the rear-view mirror. "Where to, folks? I don't go south of the river, mind."

Stick thinks. "Let's go to Supersavers. We can—"

"Shush!" squeals Nic. "The Baron is on TV!"

The kids lean in as the reporter shouts to the camera. "CHAOTIC SCENES AT THE GRAND OFFICIAL OPENING CEREMONY CONCERT OF BARON BEN'S BARGAIN BINZ MAGNIFICENT MEGA MALL WITH MORE THAN ONE PERSON RUNNING HOME TONIGHT TO HIDE FROM

THEIR NEIGHBOURS AS FOOTAGE OF THEM
CLEANING THEIR TOENAILS WITH THEIR
PARTNER'S TOOTHBRUSH IS BROADCAST
ON VIDWIRE. I CAN EXCLUSIVELY REVEAL
THAT THE HOMEBOTS HAVE BEEN SECRETLY
FILMING OUR PRIVATE LIVES WITHOUT OUR
PERMISSION. DETAILS ARE SCARCE BUT IT
APPEARS— WAIT, I'M JUST RECEIVING WORD
THAT BARON BEN IS ABOUT TO MAKE AN
OFFICIAL STATEMENT. STAND BY!"

"Looks like it worked then," says Sam.

"Look," says Alannah, "It's him."

LIVE AND EXCLUSIVE BARON BEN EXCLU

"Mr Ben—" begins the reporter.

"It's Baron Ben, actually," says the Baron, interrupting her. "And I'd just like to say on behalf of myself and Bendustries Incorporated that the clips broadcast tonight were nothing to do with me or with the company, I can very much assure you of that. This was all the work of one rogue employee who is currently being dealt with by our security team."

"Mr – er, Baron Ben, I'm sure a lot of people at home will be wondering about the surprising discovery that there are cameras in their … *our* HomeBots. What can you tell us about that?"

"Due to a manufacturing fault, some of our HomeBots may have been mistakenly fitted with cameras. The employee I mentioned took advantage of this."

"Do you know why?"

"I couldn't possibly say. This is now a matter for our security team. If you'll excuse me, I have some urgent business to attend to."

"Thank you. Well, there you have it, folks, it looks like that clears everything up. This is Dana Fitzpatrick, reporting live for Channel B News. *And now a word from our sponsor, Baron Ben's Bargain Binz!*"

"What a swizz," says Stick, slumping in his seat. "Turn it off."

"What now?" says Ekam. "He gets away with it?"

"Looks like it," says Alannah. "And Birdy takes the blame."

"All the recordings went to her blog address…" says Jazz.

"So he set her up," says Sam. "In case anything went wrong."

"So clever!" says Nic. "But evil. Also evil."

"At least people won't trust their HomeBots any more," says Ekam, as the limo pulls up outside Supersavers Superdiscount Superstore. "Look."

The kids look out at a line of customers arriving at the store. Stick's mum is standing by a makeshift sign that says 'Free HomeBot Recycling'.

Bella rolls down her window.

"Hello, Mum! Delivery for you." The back door opens, and the kids file out.

"All right, bellissima?" asks Mum, looking confused. "You're travelling in style. I thought you had a date tonight?"

"I do, Mum. See you later!" yells Bella as the limo pulls

out of the car park, leaving the kids standing there. Mum looks at the seven scruffy children in fancy dress standing in a quiet huddle, and smiles. "Are these your new friends, Stick?"

"Yes, Mum," says Stick.

"Looks like you lot have a story to tell. Why don't you come inside and get a cup of tea in the staffroom? Maybe then one of you can tell me what's going on…"

Stick wakes up really late on Sunday. He can hear the clattering of pots and his dad's voice in the kitchen, and then his mum laughing in the living room. They're both at home? Sweet. He yawns and gets up, scratching his bum as he wanders downstairs.

"Good morning, sunshine!" shouts Dad. "Sleep OK?"

"Hey, doofus," says Bella, looking up from her phone. "How are you after your awfully big adventure?"

"All right, I think," says Stick, yawning again.

"Top bunch of friends you've made there, lad," says Dad. "I like that Sam, seems like a good kid."

After Alannah had told Stick's mum the story last night, she'd called his dad to ferry everyone home in the van. "I did laugh at your theory about Bob being a spy though," he says. "Gave me a right old chuckle!"

"Yeah," says Stick. "Seems improbable."

He sits at the table with his cereal, leans his head on his hand and crunches on the chocolatey hoops. "Are you making lunch?"

"He sure is," says Mum, coming in with a cup of tea and kissing Stick on the top of his head. "So don't eat the whole box, poppet. You all right this morning?"

"Yes, Mum," says Stick, nodding and chewing.

The doorbell rings. "I'll get it," calls Bella from the stairs. "Stick, it's one of those miniature humans from last night."

Ekam appears in the kitchen with a football under his arm and a cheery smile. "Morning, all!"

The doorbell rings again and Bella answers it. "Stick, more children for you."

Nic and Milo amble in.

"Good morning, boys!" says Milo.

"Something smells good," says Nic. "What's for lunch, Mr Boy?"

The doorbell rings again and then again and soon all seven children are sitting around the kitchen table yapping and arguing about what to do next.

Sam tells them that she's had an email from Gretchen to say she's being sent to boarding school in Switzerland. Jazz says that all of Miss Bird's blogs have disappeared from the web, and Milo says that all of the ads for the HomeBot have been replaced with ads for the mayoral election and that the mall is 'closed until further notice', which makes Stick's mum smile. Alannah tells them that

Miss O'Leary has posted on the school blog that the Friday Factor final will be run again due to potential irregularities in the original results. Nic asks, again, what's for lunch. Stick sits in the middle of the racket, munching on a second bowl of cereal and looking around at his new friends. He thinks about the long days alone last summer. Ekam catches his eye from across the table and silently mouths, "All right?"

Stick smiles, and nods.

This is different.

This is good.

SPECIAL THANKS

Thank you to everyone who was a part of bringing this story
to life. To everyone at Little Tiger – to the ever-patient Ruth
for her guidance and good sense, to Sophie and Tom for their
design love and to Lauren and Leilah for letting everyone
know about our buddy Stick.

Thank you to all of you who were kind enough to read bits
of Stick's story along the way and sometimes laugh and often
say lovely things about it – Noelle and Fiachra, Clíona and
Neasa, Grace and Dan, Jason and Andra, Colum and Ruth,
Mamaí, Pop, Jay and Pravina, Lucy, Marija, Adam, Netty and
Imran, Jack, Nicola, Jamie, Karl, Rosie, Rachel, Mara, Maeve
and Mark, Aki and Alice, Matt and Meredyth and Rachel,
Alex and Lucy. And to you, dear reader, for sticking with
Stick on his little adventure.

Most of all thank you to Tanvi, an réalta is gile,
for her boundless support and inspiration.

~ LTL ~
LITTLE TOWN LIBRARY
BOOK REQUEST FORM

BOOK TITLE **The Uncommoners**
BY **JR Bell
and Karl Mountford**

BOOK TITLE **Jasper and Scruff**
BY **Nicola Colton**

BOOK TITLE **Making Comics**
BY **Scott McCloud**

BOOK TITLE **Night of the Living Ted**
BY **Barry Hutchison and
Lee Cosgrove**

BOOK TITLE **My Headteacher is an evil**
BY **Jack Noel** **genius**

BOOK TITLE **Planet Omar**
BY **Zanib Mian
Nasaya Mafaridik**

The only thing that you absolutely have to know is the location of the library.
Albert Einstein

ABOUT THE CREATOR

Paul Coomey was born in Cork, where his mother taught him to read in 1982. His favourite book that year was *Green Eggs and Ham* by Dr. Seuss, and he hasn't stopped reading since. He learned to write creatively at Kilmurry National School, where he was the only student to ever achieve a mark of 9/10 for an essay, awarded by Headmaster Der Hartnett for a story about a wolf in the snow.

When he isn't writing and illustrating books, Paul works as an Art Director in Children's Publishing. He lives in London with his wife Tanvi Kant, and in his spare time his favourite things to do are read comics and go to the sea.